The Black Pri...

A play

Iris Murdoch

Samuel French — London
New York — Sydney — Toronto — Hollywood

© 1989 BY IRIS MURDOCH

1. *This play is fully protected under the Copyright laws of the British Commonwealth of Nations, the United States of America and all countries of the Berne and Universal Copyright Conventions.*

2. *All rights including Stage, Motion Picture, Radio, Television, Public Reading, and Translation into Foreign Languages, are strictly reserved.*

---

3. **No part of this publication may lawfully be reproduced in ANY form or by any means - photocopying, typescript, recording (including video-recording), manuscript, electronic, mechanical, or otherwise - or be transmitted or stored in a retrieval system, without prior permission.**

---

4. Rights of Performance by Amateurs are controlled by Samuel French Ltd, 52 Fitzroy Street, London W1P 6JR, and they, or their authorized agents, issue licences to amateurs on payment of a fee. **It is an infringement of the Copyright to give any performance or public reading of the play before the fee has been paid and the licence issued.**

5. Licences are issued subject to the understanding that it shall be made clear in all advertising matter that the audience will witness an amateur performance; that the names of the authors of the plays shall be included on all programmes; and that the integrity of the author's work will be preserved.

   The Royalty Fee indicated below is subject to contract and subject to variation at the sole discretion of Samuel French Ltd.

   > Basic fee for each and every
   > performance by amateurs   Code M
   > in the British Isles

   In Theatres or Halls seating Six Hundred or more the fee will be subject to negotiation.

   In Territories Overseas the fee quoted above may not apply. A fee will be quoted on application to our local authorized agent, or if there is no such agent, on application to Samuel French Ltd, London.

6. The Professional Rights in this play are controlled by PETERS, FRASER & DUNLOP LTD, 5th Floor, The Chambers, Chelsea Harbour, Lots Road, London SW10 0XF

The publication of this play does not imply that it is necessarily available for performance by amateurs or professionals, either in the British Isles or Overseas. Amateurs and professionals considering a production are strongly advised in their own interests to apply to the appropriate agents for consent before starting rehearsals or booking a theatre or hall.

ISBN 0 573 01724 7

CHARACTERS

Bradley Pearson, an unsuccessful writer
Francis Marloe, a defrocked doctor
Arnold Baffin, a successful writer
Rachel Baffin, his wife
Julian Baffin, their daughter
Priscilla, Bradley Pearson's sister
Christine, Bradley Pearson's former wife
1st Policeman
2nd Policeman
Policewoman or **3rd Policeman**

The action takes place in the sitting-room of Bradley's flat, the sitting-room of Arnold's house and the sitting-room of Bradley's seaside cottage

SYNOPSIS OF SCENES

ACT I
SCENE 1   Bradley's flat
SCENE 2   Arnold's house
SCENE 3   Bradley's flat
SCENE 4   The same

ACT II
SCENE 1   The same
SCENE 2   The same

SCENE 3   Bradley's flat, Arnold's house
SCENE 4   Bradley's cottage
SCENE 5   The same
SCENE 6   Bradley's flat
SCENE 7   Arnold's house

THE BLACK PRINCE

First presented by Josephine Hart Productions Ltd, at
the Aldwych Theatre, London, on 25th April 1989,
with the following cast of characters:

Bradley Pearson	Ian McDiarmid
Francis Marloe	John Fortune
Arnold Baffin	Simon Williams
Rachel Baffin	Sarah Badel
Julian Baffin	Abigail Cruttenden
Priscilla	Norma West
Christine	Deborah Morton
1st Policeman	Peter Yapp
2nd Policeman	Christopher Mitchell
Policewoman	Norma Streader

Directed by Stuart Burge
Décor by Ultz
Lighting by Gerry Jenkinson
Music by Ilona Sekacz
Performed by the Stephen Hill Singers

ACT 1

The sitting-room of Bradley Pearson's flat

There are suitcases ready for departure. Bradley sings merry songs of liberation (such as "Linden Lea" or "Over The Hills And Far Away"). He lifts the telephone and dials

Bradley Can I have a taxi, please, to go to King's Cross Station? . . . Pearson. You know, Penrose Court. Straight away? . . . Thank you.

The doorbell rings

   Bradley goes to the door. He returns with Francis

   Who are you?

Francis I'm Francis, your brother-in-law, you know—

Bradley I have no wife, *ergo* no brother-in-law.

Francis She's back!

Bradley Who's back?

Francis Your wife, Christine, my sister, *you* know—

Bradley Christine is no longer my wife. I left her many years ago. Thank God.

Francis She's back from America, she's a widow, she's fearfully rich, don't you want to see her?

Bradley No.

Francis I'm sorry I haven't been around, you see I've been unfrocked.

Bradley I'd forgotten you were a priest. I'm afraid I've got a train to catch. I'm expecting a taxi.

Francis Not a *priest*! I'm a doctor—or I *was*—I've been struck off. Can't you remember me?

Bradley No. (*A sudden thought*). She didn't send you, did she?

Francis No, she's anti-me—don't be cross, Brad.

Bradley Don't call me "Brad"!

Francis Sorry, Brad, you see I need money, and when she comes to see you——

Bradley *What?*

Francis She really cared for you, like she loved you, she'll come.

Bradley No she won't! I'm just leaving for the country.

Francis She's rich now, *you* know, merry widow style.

Bradley I'll be away the whole summer. I'm going to write a *book.*

Francis She'll be after you, she'll want to show off, she'll come to gloat over you.

Bradley "Gloat"? What do you mean "gloat"?

Francis I've always liked you, Bradley, I've always admired you, I've read one of your books.

Bradley I haven't published any books!

Francis I forget its name, it was great—look, I'm in debt up to the neck, and when you see Christine you could——

Bradley No!

Francis With Chris back, it's like a new start, all sins forgiven.

The doorbell rings

Bradley No! Go away!

The telephone rings. Bradley picks it up. He points Francis to go to the door

Francis goes

Hello. Arnold, what's the matter? . . . *What?* . . . Impossible . . . You've killed her!? Don't be silly . . . You can't have killed her, you just can't have . . . Have you called a doctor? No? . . . What happened? . . . All right, I'll come round, I'll come at once . . .

Francis returns

Bradley replaces the receiver

Francis There's a taxi——What's up?

Bradley The wife of a friend of mine has had a serious accident, I'm just going over——

Francis Can I come?

Bradley No.

Francis I'm still a doctor in the eyes of God.

Bradley Yes—all right. Hold the taxi.

Francis goes

Bradley automatically picks up his suitcases, then puts them down

(*As the scene changes*) Arnold Baffin. The famous writer. He always exaggerates. I discovered him, I encouraged him. Now he's a book-a-year man. I'm not envious, I'm just not that kind of scribbler.

SCENE 2

The sitting-room in Arnold Baffin's house

The room is in chaos, chairs overturned, books on the floor

Rachel, lying on a sofa, looks dramatically dead, head thrown back, arm drooping to the floor

Bradley Oh my God.

Arnold She was crying and screaming.

Bradley Dr Marloe—Arnold Baffin. He happened to be with me when you rang up about your wife's *accident*.

Francis Are you *the* Arnold Baffin?

Bradley Yes, he is.
Francis I do so admire your books, I've read several of them . . .
Arnold Oh thank you.
Bradley Arnold, just keep calm——
Arnold (*distraught*) She just lies there and doesn't move and I can't bear to look at her——
Bradley Arnold, sit down.

Francis watches with interest. Arnold sits, head in hands. Bradley goes to Rachel, kneels, takes her hand

Rachel, Rachel—it's me—Bradley. Oh dear. Her hand is so cold and——
Arnold (*moaning*) Oh, let her be all right . . .
Bradley Rachel—it's Bradley—she's moving, she's looking at me!

Faint moan from Rachel

Listen, she made a sound.
Arnold (*jumping up*) Oh darling, are you all right?
Bradley Just keep away.
Arnold I'm so sorry—oh my darling——
Bradley Rachel, dear Rachel, don't worry, we'll make you better. (*To Francis*) Look, you take over.

Bradley returns to Arnold. Francis fusses over Rachel, who is showing more signs of life

Arnold Is that chap a medical doctor?
Bradley Yes.
Arnold I thought he might be a doctor of literature. Look, let's have a drink. Oh God, I've been a bloody fool.

With shaking hand Arnold pours out whisky for himself. From now on Arnold begins to recover, perhaps regrets having panicked so soon and invited his friend into this domestic scene

Bradley What happened?
Arnold We had a damn stupid argument about one of my books—she thinks, or says she thinks, they're all about *her*, all caricatures of *her*.
Francis (*coming forward*) First-aid kit? Hot water, basin, towels?
Arnold (*pointing*) Kitchen. Is she OK?
Francis Hope so.

Francis goes

Arnold I thought she was done for. Silly of me to panic. She gets this persecution mania—I said a few things and then we just couldn't stop, she began to scream and I can't *stand* that, and I pushed her and she clawed my face—here, see—and I slapped her and then she sprang on me like a tiger and I picked up this poker just to keep her away, like a barrier between us, I didn't mean to hit her, I mean, I didn't hit her, and then suddenly she was pouring blood——

Francis appears, drying his hands on a towel

Francis Nothing serious—a cut on the head, a lot of bruising, very nasty fall she must have had. I think her nose is OK.

Arnold I'm so grateful——

Francis Bit of concussion and shock. You'd better get your own doctor. (*To Bradley*) She wants to see you, not him.

Arnold Oh my sweetheart, don't be angry with me!

Bradley You two clear off.

Francis and Arnold depart. Francis seizes the whisky bottle as he goes

Bradley goes to Rachel, who has come forward

There, my dear, there now, you'll be all right.

Rachel is a sad sight, blood, black eye. She feels her nose carefully and round her eye. She is not crying now. She speaks in a fierce cold voice, not looking at Bradley

Rachel No I won't be all right.

Bradley Of course you will!

Rachel It's the shame, it's the disgrace—and he invited you round to see it!

Bradley He was shaking like a leaf. He was afraid he'd hurt you.

Rachel Hurt me! He's taken my whole life and blackened it and stolen it and put it into his hateful lying books. *And* he discusses me with other women, everybody loves him and flatters him, he's surrounded by women. Be my witness, I shall never forgive him, never, never, never, not if he were to kneel at my feet for twenty years. If he were drowning I'd watch, I'd *laugh*.

Bradley Rachel, please don't talk in this awful theatrical way. You don't mean it, don't say it! Of course, you'll forgive him!

Rachel I'm just as clever as he is—but I can't work, I can't think, I can't *be* because of him. I've never lived my own life at all, I've always been afraid of him, that's what it comes to. All men despise all women really, all women fear all men really. Men are physically stronger, that's what it comes to. They can end an argument! He's given me a black eye, just like any common drunken lout——

Bradley I'm sure there were faults on both sides.

Rachel I'm a battered wife.

Bradley But you hit him.

Rachel Ach! And he's hit me before! I never told him, but the first time he hit me our marriage came to an end. He has taken away my life and spoilt it, breaking every little piece of it, like breaking every bone in one's body, every little thing ruined and spoilt and *stolen*.

Bradley Rachel, don't talk like this, I won't listen.

Rachel He wouldn't let me take a job. I obeyed him, I've always obeyed him! I haven't any private things. He owns the world. It's all his, his! I won't save him at the end. I'll watch him drown, I'll watch him burn.

Bradley Oh, Rachel——

Rachel And I won't forgive you either for seeing me like this with my face all bruised and my eyes running with tears.

Bradley Rachel you're upsetting me!

Rachel And now you'll go and comfort him and connive with him and tell him all the dreadful things I've said.

Bradley No I won't!

Rachel I fill you with disgust and contempt—a battered whimpering middle-aged woman. Now I'm going upstairs to bed. Just tell Arnold not to come near me. I'll come down later, I'll be as usual, I'll be myself. Myself, ha! (*She starts to go*)

Bradley Don't be cross with me, it's not my fault!

Rachel departs. A distant door slams

Poor old Rachel. And it's not the end of that either. (*He turns to the audience*) My life before it was enlivened by these events had been a quiet one. Some people might call it dull. In fact, if one can use that rather beautiful and pungent word in an almost non-emotive sense, my life had been sublimely dull. A great dull life—spent working as a Tax Inspector. A great Danish philosopher once described the truly virtuous man as "looking like an Inspector of Taxes". More usually, and perhaps this is the point, a taxman is a figure of fun. The profession like that of dentist, invites laughter. But this laughter is, I suspect, uneasy. Both taxman and dentist only too readily image forth the deeper horrors of human life; that we must pay for our pleasures, that our resources are lent, not given, and that our faculties decay even as they grow. My life since—all this (*a gesture*) has been secluded, solitary. I have in my monastic enclosure become more happy, I hope more wise . . . This direct speaking is a kind of relief. It eases some pressure upon the heart, allowing the mind to pass like a light along a series of present moments aware of past images, unaware of what is to come. I am a writer, a serious writer, that is an artist. If someone complains, but you have published nothing! I reply: that is the essence. I am not a blocked writer, I am a perfectionist—a slave of the dark power which alone enables beauty to be truth. In art, as in lives of men, great things are lost because at the crucial moment, when the empowered imagination is poised for its final work, we let go, we think, "that'll do", and we accept the second best. When is that moment? Greatness is to recognize it, to hold it, to extend it (*he gestures*). The most sacred command laid upon any artist is: wait. Writing is like getting married. Don't commit yourself until you are amazed at your luck.

Arnold and Francis return, carrying bottles and glasses

She's gone to bed. She says please leave her alone, she'll be down later.

Arnold God, what a relief. I expect she'll be down for supper. I'll cook her something special.

Bradley All the same it was a serious accident.

Arnold He says she'll recover quickly. Have another drink.

Bradley I haven't had one yet. (*To Francis*) Well, we needn't keep you, thank you for helping.

Arnold Oh, don't go, Doctor!

Bradley (*firmly*) Goodbye.
Arnold I'm so grateful—do I owe you anything?
Bradley You owe him nothing.

Francis is very reluctant to go. He drains his glass. Bradley begins to shepherd him out

Francis Better keep her in bed. (*To Bradley*) About what we said before—when you see Christine——
Bradley I won't.
Francis Here's my address. (*He thrusts it into Bradley's hand*)
Bradley Goodbye, thank you.

Francis departs

Arnold fills his own glass. They continue to drink during the conversation which follows

Do you really think she'll come down to supper?
Arnold Yes, she never sulks for long. These rows aren't real warfare, we love each other. My hand is trembling—look at the way that glass is shaking—it's quite involuntary—isn't it odd?
Bradley You'd better get your own doctor in tomorrow.
Arnold Oh I shall be all right tomorrow. You know I think she was shamming a bit to frighten me.
Bradley Do you mind if I tidy up?

Bradley puts chairs upright, returns books to the bookcase

Arnold We're happily married. I'm not a violent person. But marriage is a long journey. Of course we argue. Every married person is a Jekyll and Hyde really. You know, Rachel is a real nagger. She can go on and on saying the same thing over and over, I mean repeating the same sentence.
Bradley Then she should see a psychiatrist.
Arnold That shows you've no idea! Half an hour later she's singing in the kitchen.
Bradley She said you discussed her with other women. You're not playing around?
Arnold No, I'm a model husband! Why shouldn't I talk to women, I have to have friends, I can't give way on a point like that—it could be a very serious sacrifice—and if a sacrifice would make you mad with resentment you oughtn't to make it!
Bradley Naturally I won't mention this business to anybody.
Arnold (*glancing at Bradley, a bit annoyed*) Oh—well—suit yourself. Why did you chuck that doctor out so quickly? He said he was your friend.
Bradley Did he! Well, he's not!
Arnold He said something about Christine—wasn't that your wife?
Bradley Ex-wife. He's her brother.
Arnold How awfully interesting! Isn't she in America? She married an American. I wish I'd met her.

Bradley She's in London now, she's a rich widow.

Arnold So you'll see her?

Bradley No, why should I? I don't like her.

Arnold Hurt pride?

Bradley Hurt pride! No, *I* left *her*.

Arnold Well, resentment.

Bradley Hatred, my dear Arnold, pure mutual hatred.

Arnold I don't believe in hatred, I think it's terribly rare. I should be dying with curiosity if I were you. So the doctor is her brother——

Bradley He's not a doctor, he was struck off.

Arnold Ex-wife, ex-doctor! What did he do?

Bradley I don't know, I don't like him either.

Arnold You mustn't be so censorious. I rather liked him actually, I asked him to come round and see us.

Bradley Oh no . . .!

Arnold You ought to be interested in people and know details about them, justice demands details. Curiosity is a kind of charity.

Bradley I think curiosity is a kind of malice.

Arnold That's what makes a writer, knowing details.

Bradley It may be your sort of writer, it doesn't make mine!

Arnold Here we go again!

Bradley Malicious sketches and lists of things one happens to have noticed isn't art!

Arnold I never said it was—I don't draw directly from life!

Bradley Your wife thinks so.

Arnold (*dismissive gesture*) Oh . . .!

Bradley Journalistic reportage isn't art, and neither is semi-pornographic romantic fantasy! Art is truth, art is imagination, it's metamorphosis, without that you have either senseless details or egotistic dreams.

Arnold (*raising his voice*) All right!

Bradley Art comes out of endless restraint plus silence.

Arnold If the silence is endless there isn't any art!

Bradley One must wait for what's perfect——

Arnold I publish things without waiting for them to be perfect because I know they'll never be perfect, anything else is hypocrisy—that's what it means to be a professional writer. Why not just think of yourself as someone who very occasionally writes something, who may in the future write something? Why make a life drama out of it?

Bradley Are you suggesting I'm some sort of amateur?

Arnold I know I'm second rate, I live with continual failure, every book is the wreck of a good idea! But there's no point in moaning about it—if you publish a book it must look after itself. I don't think I'd write better if I wrote less, I'd just be less happy.

Bradley grimaces

I enjoy writing, it's a natural function. The alternative is to be like you, finish nothing, publish nothing, have a grudge against the whole world, and feel superior to people who try and fail!

Bradley How clearly you put it, my dear fellow.

Julian enters. She is wearing a track-suit and carrying a cassette player with headphones

Bradley and Arnold exchange signals

Julian Hello Bradley.

Arnold Hello darling. You haven't seen your mother have you? I'll just pop up, she's not well.

Arnold goes

Julian They were quarrelling so I left the house. Have they calmed down?

Bradley Yes of course.

Julian Don't you think they quarrel more than they used to?

Bradley No!

Julian I'm so glad you're here, I want to ask you something. (*She tears up a letter*)

Bradley What are you doing?

Julian It's a love-letter from my ex-boyfriend.

Bradley Have you parted company?

Julian Yes, here goes the last I hope. (*She puts it in the waste-paper basket*) That's better. I want your advice about something.

Bradley What?

Arnold enters

Or is it a secret?

Arnold She's asleep.

Julian I've decided to become a writer, and I want you to help me.

Groans from Bradley and Arnold

Bradley (*pointing to Arnold*) There's the expert!

Julian Fathers can't teach—and anyway I think I'm going to be your kind of writer, not Daddy's kind.

Bradley (*amused*) What is my kind?

Julian The slow kind.

Bradley and Arnold laugh

Julian skips out

Arnold Bradley—we mustn't be enemies, we *mustn't* be—Not just because it's nicer to be at peace, but because we could do serious damage to each other—we know exactly what hurts the other most.

Bradley (*making to go*) I couldn't damage anybody. I just want to get my book written.

Arnold (*getting a book*) By the way, here's my latest novel, with the usual affectionate inscription. Someone told me you were reviewing it?

Bradley, accepting the novel, politely signifies assent

Why don't you come to lunch next week? Rachel would love to see you.

Bradley Would she? Next week I shall be over the hills and far away. I've left the old Tax Office, I'm a free man!

Arnold Of course, that cottage by the sea where you're going to write your great book. Where is it?

Bradley That's a secret! (*To the audience*) I had at various times tried quite hard to reflect rationally upon the value of Arnold's work. I think I objected to him most because he was such a "gabbler". He wrote very carelessly, of course. But the gabble was not just casual and slipshod, it was an aspect of what one might call his "metaphysic". Arnold was always trying, as it were, to take over the world by emptying himself over it like scented bath water.

SCENE 3

Bradley's flat

Bradley is on the phone

Bradley Can I have a taxi, please, to go to King's Cross Station? . . . Pearson. You know, Penrose Court. Straight away? . . . Thank you.

The front doorbell rings

Damn!

Bradley goes to the door and admits Priscilla. She walks in, and starts to cry

Priscilla! What's the matter? For God's sake—what is it?

Priscilla I've left my husband.

Bradley Bloody Roger—I'm not surprised. Yes, I am surprised! Don't be silly, you can't have left him, you've had some little tiff—it's the hot weather.

Priscilla My marriage is over, my life is over, I'm dead, I'm dried up, I'm *shrivelled* with misery and grief, years and years of misery and grief.

Bradley Priscilla, I'm terribly sorry, but I am just at this moment leaving London. I've just rung for a taxi.

Priscilla You're my brother, you've got to help me, someone's got to help me. I don't know how a human being can be so unhappy all the time and still be alive (*a sob*). Roger has become a devil, he wants to kill me, he tried to poison me.

Bradley Oh nonsense——

Priscilla Living with someone who hates you drives you mad. He said I was mad and he'd have me certified. I put up with it because there was nothing else to do.

Bradley Priscilla, there *is* nothing else to do! Roger's a very selfish nasty man, but you'll just have to forgive him! You can't leave him, you haven't anywhere else to go.

Priscilla I got rid of the child because he said he couldn't afford it and then I couldn't have another.

Bradley Please, not that old story! Look, I've got a train to catch.

Priscilla I've never felt well since, never. I think I've got cancer. Can I have a drink? I've started drinking. That's another thing he holds against me.

Bradley brings a sherry bottle and glass, pours some. Priscilla takes off her shoes, then her jacket and skirt. Bradley watches with dismay as she begins to settle herself on the sofa

Could you put a rug over me?

Bradley puts a rug over her. Priscilla sips the sherry, then petulantly returns it to Bradley

No, don't touch me, I can't bear to be touched, I feel like a leper, I feel my flesh is rotting. Do I smell terrible? I wish I was a corpse, a dead one not a living one. He cut down my magnolia tree, the garden was *his* garden, the house was *his* house, I gave him my life, I haven't got another one. Oh, I'm so *frightened*.

Bradley (*to the audience*) My parents kept a stationer's shop in Croydon. My sister Priscilla and I slept under the counter. No, of course we didn't, we can't have done—but I remember it all the same. Some people just have rotten lives. Why did God love Jacob and hate Esau? Answer me that one! Take Priscilla for instance. My mother certainly hated Priscilla. Well, she hated me too, but I hated her so it didn't signify. (*To Priscilla*) Priscilla, listen, I'm going away—you can't stay here!

Priscilla Roger hated the sight of me, he said so. And I used to cry in front of him, I'd sit and cry for hours with sheer misery, and he'd just go on reading the paper.

Bradley You make me feel quite sorry for him!

Priscilla Oh I know I've lost my looks——

Bradley As if that mattered!

Priscilla So you think I look horrible? Ach—I made a home for that man, I tried and tried, when he shouted at me I asked him to forgive me! I kept trying to make everything nice for him, to keep the house nice and now I've left it all behind, all my things, my nice *things*, my fur coat, my pearls, my amber necklace, and my little ornaments, the little animals I had, my Chinese vases and the silver looking-glass and the ducks—all my nice things, all gone.

Bradley They're perfectly safe at home!

Priscilla No they're not! There is no home. Please, please, could you go and fetch them. He'll destroy them all out of spite. I'm a fool, I just ran out—I hate Roger, I hate him, I'd like to stick a red-hot knitting-needle into his liver.

Bradley Priscilla!

Priscilla I read it in a detective story. You die slowly in terrible agony.

Bradley Do stop this!

Priscilla You don't understand, you don't see the horror, no wonder you can't write books, you've had an easy life, you've never had this sort of pain, oh the pain, if you only knew what it's like to be me, to want to spend hours and hours just screaming with pain . . . (*She begins to utter little hysterical moaning cries*)

Bradley Oh shut up! You can't stay here!

Priscilla I'll kill myself—that's best—they'll say she's better dead—she had too much pain—and now it's over—she's dead, she's DEAD.

The doorbell rings

Bradley Oh God, the taxi——

Bradley goes to the door

Priscilla produces a bottle of pills from her handbag and swallows handfuls of them with gulps of sherry

Bradley returns

Now just stop all this——

Priscilla (*calmly*) Don't worry—I've just eaten all my sleeping pills.

Bradley I don't believe you——

Priscilla Eaten them all—see? (*She shows the empty bottle*) Now you can go away. Just leave me alone—and I'll go to sleep—and forget it all—forever—it's the end, it's the end. (*She drops the bottle on the floor and covers her face with the rug*)

Bradley Oh God—Priscilla! (*He rushes to and fro; lifts the telephone; fumbles with telephone directories*) Now you've made me miss my train.

The doorbell rings

Bradley goes out and then returns with Francis

Francis I hope you don't mind my coming.

Bradley No, I don't!

Francis *What?*

Bradley My sister has just taken an overdose of sleeping pills—she's under that rug.

Francis removes the rug and inspects Priscilla who moans slightly

Francis Try to get her sitting up. What did she take? Can you find the bottle?

Bradley It was here just now . . .

During what follows Francis carries on a sort of struggle with Priscilla who is moaning and throwing herself about

Francis Ring up Middlesex Hospital and ask for Casualty. How many did you take? Tell me what you took.

Priscilla gags. The doorbell rings

Arnold and Rachel enter. They are in their best clothes and look like a model pair in an advertisement except that Rachel has a slightly black eye. They stand together and click their heels and salute, smiling at Bradley

Arnold You left the door open so we came in. We thought we'd come and parade ourselves, it's such a lovely warm day. We want to show you how all right we are, and wish you *bon voyage* and the best of luck with the book!

Arnold ⎱
Rachel ⎰ (*together*) *Bon voyage* and best of luck with the book!

Bradley My sister Priscilla has just attempted suicide.

Exclamations of appalled sympathy

Francis Where's the bottle?
Bradley I've got to find the bottle. (*He starts crawling about the floor*)
Arnold What bottle? We'll help!

They all help

Francis Ring up the hospital!
Bradley Rachel, could you do it? Ring the Middlesex hospital and ask for Casualty and tell them——
Rachel Yes—yes——
Priscilla Help me, help me to die.
Francis You're not going to die.

Rachel seizes the telephone book from Bradley. During the following exchanges her voice continues semi-audibly, sometimes covered by the other speeches. An effect of everyone talking at once

Arnold Francis, my dear old friend, always where the action is!
Rachel Casualty please, yes, urgent.
Priscilla (*in the background*) Help me—help me to die—oh help me to die.
Rachel Someone has taken an overdose of sleeping pills.

Julian enters

Julian What's happened? Dad, what's happened?
Arnold (*searching*) The bottle, the bottle.
Julian (*to Bradley*) Is someone hurt?
Bradley No, yes, my sister, that's my sister. We've got to find the bottle!
Julian Oh dear! What bottle?
Priscilla Can't you please just let me die?
Arnold (*finding the bottle*) Is this it?

Francis comes forward and takes the bottle

Francis Brad! Some salty water.

Bradley goes to fetch it

Rachel I can't hear—(*To the others*) Be quiet! (*Shouting to Bradley*) When did she take them?
Bradley (*off*) Just now.
Rachel Just now. . . . Yes—yes . . .
Priscilla Bradley, you won't leave me, will you, you'll go and get my things——

Rachel Twenty-three Penrose Court—you know—yes . . .
Priscilla I haven't anyone but you, you won't leave me alone, will you . . .
Bradley (*off*) Of course not.
Rachel That's right, we're quite close.
Priscilla I'm so unhappy . . .

   Bradley returns with a glass of water

Bradley Stop jumping about, can't you *rest*?
Priscilla *Rest!*
Rachel (*finishing the phone call*) Yes—thank you so much. (*To Francis*)
   I'm so grateful to you.
Francis (*pleased*) Not at all, it was a pleasure.

The doorbell rings

Rachel It can't be the ambulance already.
Priscilla Don't leave me!
Arnold I'll go.

   Arnold and Rachel go out to the front door

Francis returns to Priscilla. Bradley comes forward, holding his head

Julian Bradley, I'm so sorry. Poor Priscilla, oh dear, old age is so awful.
Bradley (*raised eyebrows, curtly*) Yes. Isn't it. (*Distractedly he tidies the
   scene, picking up Priscilla's skirt and shoes*)
Julian But she'll be all right, won't she?
Bradley Yes, yes.
Julian Bradley, I'm sorry to be a bother, can I ask you something?
Bradley (*distracted*) What?
Julian Could you do something for me?
Bradley Oh God, why does this have to happen!
Julian Could you talk to me a bit about *Hamlet*?
Bradley *Hamlet*?
Julian I don't mean now. What about Tuesday at eleven, here. You see
   it's my set book for my exam. It's such a *confusing* play—Do you think
   Gertrude was in league with Claudius to kill the king?
Bradley No.
Julian I thought perhaps she was having an affair with Claudius before
   the king died?
Bradley No.
Julian You don't think that all women at a certain age feel an urge to
   commit adultery . . . ?
Bradley No.

Sounds of ambulance

   Rachel returns

She helps Francis to get Priscilla to her feet and propel her towards the door

Rachel Ambulance.

Priscilla Nobody loves me, nobody cares about me. My mother hated me, my father hated. They broke my back, they broke my bones.

Bradley God, I hope she'll be all right.

Priscilla (*at the door*) I don't exist, I've never existed. I'm nothing— nothing . . .

Her wails die away outside, as Rachel and Francis lead her out, wrapped in a rug

Bradley Wait a moment, what about her clothes! (*He rushes to Julian carrying Priscilla's jacket, skirt, shoes*)

Julian goes with them. During this confusion, Arnold has returned, unnoticed by Bradley, with Christine. She looks youthful and smart, and speaks with a slight American accent

(*To Arnold*) What's the matter with you? (*Noticing Christine*) Christine!

Christine Bradley—after all these years, the same old Bradley, I thought you might be old and grey, but you're *young*—isn't he young——?

Rachel enters

Rachel Francis has gone with her, she'll be fine. (*She sits on the sofa*)

Christine And poor old Priscilla, I remember Priscilla—oh the poor thing. Isn't it just a cry for help, Rachel?

Julian enters

And this is your lovely daughter. Hi Julian!

Julian Hi.

Bradley (*utterly confused*) But—do you all know each other?

Christine Yes, we do!—We met on the doorstep. Say, I like your friends. (*Indicating Arnold*) I've read all his books, isn't that great? (*To Arnold*) I wrote an essay on you when I was a mature student.

Arnold You must come round and see us.

Rachel Yes, do come!

Arnold and Rachel are thoroughly amused by this scene, so far

Christine I'd love to—I don't have any friends in London now, I don't know anybody except him (*indicating Bradley*) and my delinquent brother—he came round to my place yesterday asking for money and now it turns out he's a friend of you—all—it's a small world, that's for sure. Bradley—(*she stares at him with appreciation, head on one side*) well, well, it's like old times . . .

Arnold May we offer Christine a drink? (*He does so, getting glasses from the cupboard and seizing the sherry bottle*)

Julian Bradley, I have to go.

Christine Oh.

Julian Tuesday will be OK, won't it?

Julian exits

Christine Brad, you're all of a tremble!

Bradley (*to Christine*) Will you please leave my house?

Christine Bradley, please don't take that tone. I've been thinking about is all—I come in peace.

Arnold Bradley, relax, you've got to face it, it's got to happen——

Christine It's happening. I'm all of a tremble too. I'm in a state of shock. You know I pictured this meeting a thousand times, I dreamt about it, I thought I'd faint! And now—it's a blessed miracle. Brad, dear, do say something—say something kind and good!

Bradley I have written you a letter. Here it is.

He hands the letter to Christine who reads it

Christine Well, it's not very polite! (*She hands the letter to Arnold*)

Arnold (*reading*) "I do not under *any circumstances wish to see you*. Do not, prompted by curiosity or morbid interest attempt to . . . In the long years of our merciful separation I have forgotten you . . ."

Christine Of course he hasn't! (*She peers at the letter too*)

Arnold (*touching her sleeve and reading on*) "I was relieved to be rid of you, I do not like you. But since your memories of me are doubtless as disagreeable as my memories of you . . ."

Christine But they're not disagreeable, that's what I came to say! You mustn't be scared.

Bradley I am not scared!

Christine Well, you're all sort of excited—isn't he excited?

Arnold (*very amused*) Oh Bradley, what a writer you are, it's a real writer's letter! Listen to this.

Bradley Shut up!

Christine Jesus, I shall get the giggles—I always do when I'm shit scared. (*Indicating Arnold*) You know this man makes me laugh! Oh Lordie!

Arnold is laughing quietly over Bradley's letter. Christine begins to giggle. He and Christine go off into crazy laughter

Rachel (*now uneasy*) Bradley, I'm sorry. Don't worry about Priscilla. Come on, Arnold, we must go too.

Arnold I'm going to stay with Bradley, I think he needs a friend!

Christine I could look after Priscilla. I know all about suicide, My God, I did a course. I'll go see her.

Bradley Oh no you won't.

Christine Don't get so het up, man. Let's talk.

Bradley I refer you to my letter.

Christine (*to Arnold*) You say something to him.

Arnold much amused, makes despairing gestures. Christine laughs. She turns to Bradley

Come now. I'm glad to see you. I thought you'd be glad to see me. I pictured your eyes all warm and smiling. Was I crazy? Maybe it's just that I'm happy now. I get a buzz from the whole world, I love everything. I wake in the morning and I cry Hallelujah! (*Turning to

Arnold) Am I awful? You see I'm free now, I'm a free lady. Like in Zen when you get enlightenment.

Arnold Satori! I know all about Buddhism.

Christine (*to Arnold*) I guess I went through Zen like a knife through butter. I'm into real philosophy now—Goodness Ethics.

Arnold Aren't all ethics goodness ethics?

Christine (*counting on her fingers*) Oh no—there's Duty Ethics, and Virtue Ethics, and Welfare Ethics—But Goodness Ethics is the new Christianity. God is out, he's right out, he's finished. That leaves Jesus, sort of like Buddha, you can have him for free, no need to believe in all that old stuff. (*She points upward*) It's all here and now! You take Jesus as your Saviour, and Jesus equals Goodness, so you just *love* Goodness, like in Plato!

Rachel Plato!

Arnold That sounds wonderful, we must discuss it, I'm so interested in religion.

Christine (*to Bradley*) He's laughing at me, but it's all true!

Bradley You came here to exhibit your self-satisfaction, your fancy American accent and your money, and now that you have done so will you kindly understand that I do not want to see you.

Christine What's wrong with being rich? It's a quality, it's attractive. Rich people are nicer, they're less nervy, they're serene. Look, I come back here and I come straight to you. Think about that. I'm not an emotional kid looking for kicks. I'm a middle-aged well-balanced woman. I can see into my motivation. I was years in deep analysis back in Illinois. I want real happiness. I want friendship, I want to know all sorts of people, I want to help people. I guess it would help us if we could discuss our marriage, so we could sort of redeem the past.

Bradley You make me sick——

Christine Say, have you been analysed?

Bradley *Analysed?!*

Christine Lie down, relax, and talk about yourself to a nice wise Jew, it's great. That's what you need! (*To Arnold*) Don't you agree?

Bradley And leave my friends alone!

Christine Oh come on, Brad, you don't own your friends. You're getting jealous already! (*To Arnold*) He always was a jealous man. (*To Bradley*) How many books have you published? I thought you'd be a real author by now. We had a literary guy from England to our Writer's Circle, but he hadn't heard of you. Say, it's great to meet Arnold Baffin though. You still in the old Tax Office?

Arnold He's retired.

Christine I've got some dandy tax problems. I thought maybe you'd help me. (*To Arnold*) He never should have been in that office, he ought to have been out seeing the real world, no wonder he can't write. I've seen plenty and I'll see plenty more. I always wanted to be an authoress, I did a course in creative writing and——

Bradley (*pointing to the door*) Will you get out?

Christine Bradley, don't be unkind to me—don't you think I might be a different person now?

Bradley I am not interested in anything you might have become.

Arnold Of course he's interested! Bradley don't be so pompous and vindictive!

Bradley gestures towards the door

Christine All right, buster, if that's the way you want it. I thought maybe we could have some fun together, you and me. I'm a rich woman now, I'm going to be happy and I'm going to make other folks happy. I've been looking at you, Bradley Pearson, and you're not a happy man.

Bradley I may not be happy, but I'm not for sale. Go away I hate you. I just simply hate you.

Christine Bradley, hatred's bad, it's negative.

Bradley points again at the door. Christine makes a wry face and a helpless gesture. She repeats the gesture to Arnold. She waves to Rachel, who is still sitting on the sofa

Bye!

Christine goes out

Arnold galvanized, starts to go after her, then turns back

Arnold Bradley . . .

Bradley regards him grimly

Arnold with a quick glance at Rachel runs out after Christine

Silence while Bradley and Rachel, not looking at each other, breathe deeply

Rachel (*still sitting at the back*) Well, that was an interesting scene.

Bradley Hatred is terrible, it's degrading . . .

Rachel I don't think it's degrading, it's a natural phenomenon. It's a source of energy.

Bradley (*absorbed in his rage and misery*) That woman gets right inside me, it's like swallowing a knife. But no-one seems to want to believe that I really do hate her!

Rachel I believe it. I know hatred.

Bradley She's the only person I hate. Because of her I know about hatred, and I don't like it. Being infuriated with Arnold is something quite different. God, I must calm down! I've written a nasty review of his new novel, I can't decide whether to publish it. (*He takes the review from his pocket and reads*) Listen to this. "Arnold Baffin's new novel provides his many admirers with what they want, the mixture as before. Hero, stockbroker, forty, decides to become a monk, enters monastery. Heroine, sister of Abbot, intense lady returned from East, tries to convert hero to Buddhism. Boring ill-informed discussion of comparative religion." (Oh for a little light relief!) "Abbot" (Christ figure of course) "is killed by immense bronze crucifix falling on his head. Is it an accident?" etc. etc. (*Skipping*) "Mr Baffin is a fluent prolific writer, this facility, which he mistakes for imagination, is his worst enemy. A good writer needs the courage to destroy and to wait. Judging by his output, Mr Baffin is incapable of either destroying or waiting. Only a genius can afford 'never to blot a line'. We must ask of this book, not whether it is entertaining, but whether it is a work of art. The answer is, alas, no. Naturally the film rights have already been sold."

Rachel (*peering at the review*) It's perfectly horrid, it's spiteful, you can't publish that!

Bradley makes as if to crumple it up, then restores it to his pocket

Actually you're in love with Arnold, everybody is, you're a masochist, you like it when he puts you down.

Bradley I do not!

Rachel He's very fond of you. So is Julian. She admires you because you're so unlike Dad, she says she's been trying to attract your attention for years. I wish you'd see her sometime. She's awfully unhappy, poor child.

Bradley It's an unhappy age, always falling in love. Thank God I'm past it.

Rachel Are you? I see you as all set to fall in love all over again with Christine.

Bradley (*controlled*) Rachel, dear, don't make me *scream!*

Rachel She's awfully clever and attractive. I think Arnold's fallen for her already.

Bradley No!!

Rachel What do you imagine he's doing now? He's sitting with her in some pub, then he'll give her lunch, then they'll go back to her flat, and he'll make her tell him everything about your marriage.

Bradley Let me not be mad, not mad, sweet heavens!

Rachel (*cool, tormenting him*) Arnold makes people talk, he's everybody's father confessor. She'll be dying to tell him the details of how awful it was.

Bradley If Arnold were to . . . with Christine . . .

Rachel I know, you'd kill him. Perhaps we need to *imagine* things like that to stop us actually murdering our nearest and dearest. Calm down, Bradley, remember you're a quiet timid man. It's all in your head.

Bradley I live in my head. (*He suddenly seizes Arnold's new novel which is lying on the table and tears it to pieces*) Sorry.

Rachel (*kicking the pieces away*) Don't worry, I enjoyed that. Really, about Arnold and his women, I'm a bit relieved, it helps me to feel free. Let's have a drink.

Bradley I'm always drinking these days. I don't usually. God, and there's poor Priscilla, I must ring up——

Rachel pours a drink for herself and Bradley

Rachel Bradley, sit down.

They sit side by side

Bradley I thought you might hate the sight of me because I came—you know, on that day . . .

Rachel No, it makes me feel closer to you. I've always wanted to know you better, but I've felt shy. You're a *difficult* man.

Bradley (*gratified*) Am I?

Rachel I imagine it's a long time since you made love to a woman.

Bradley Yes. (*Pregnant pause*) Look, I really must ring the hospital . . .

He is reaching for the telephone when it rings

Yes. . . . (*To Rachel*) It's Francis. Yes, Francis. She's all right, no danger at all? . . . Thank heavens for that. . . . Yes, I'll fetch her bloody things . . . she's made a list, has she! . . . Good! . . . Thank you. . . . I'll be along. (*He replaces the receiver*) I think I'd better—go and see her . . .

Bradley is clearly uncertain about whether he wants to sit down again beside Rachel or to run away to see Priscilla. Rachel firmly pats the sofa and he returns to his seat

Rachel Bradley, I knew she'd be all right. Do you mind if I kiss you? I've always wanted to give you a real kiss, not just a social kiss. (*She kisses him*) Bradley—dear . . .

Bradley Thank you. But—look—I'm a lone wolf——

Rachel I've only kissed you! You *are* racing ahead! Or do you think women of my age have a sudden urge——?

Bradley Like Gertrude. No.

Rachel Who's Gertrude?

Bradley Old flame of mine. I just mean I don't want any muddle.

Rachel You mean like falling in love with *me*?

Bradley (*calmly*) No. It's just that I've got work to do. I've got to be alone. I'm going to write a book I've been waiting all my life to write.

Rachel Don't be so solemn about your book, it won't do it any good! You musn't think of yourself as a writer, like Arnold, you must just write. You need *more life* and that's what I need too. Now hold my hand, that's right, I won't harm you, Bradley, it's all *simple*. I need love, I need more people to love, I need you to love. I think you need me to love. I've been so tired—and motionless—I must move, I must have new feelings. That won't hurt Arnold, he'll be glad—I've become a dull wife. Listen, concentrate, you're good for me, you're the only person with whom I'm not acting a part!

Bradley I'm glad—but——

Rachel We may even have found a key to happiness—one can't really be happy until one's over forty. My dear, don't look like that, I don't mean dramas or adventures or crises, we must just come closer, you must let me love you.

Bradley But do you mean something secret? I don't like secrets.

Rachel No, Arnold will know, everyone will know, that we care for each other a bit specially—but—well—any close friendship is secret too. You do love me a bit, don't you?

Bradley Of course, I always have, but I can't exactly define——
Rachel Don't define! That's the point!
Bradley Rachel, I don't want to feel guilty, it would interfere with my work.
Rachel (*a little laugh*) Oh, you're such a puritan! (*She slips off her jacket*)
Bradley I'm terrified of being tied to anything just now, I've got to write this book and I've got to be *worthy* of it.
Rachel Bradley, I do admire you, you're so much more serious about writing than Arnold is. But why can't you write? It's because you're *repressed*, I mean in a spiritual way.
Bradley In a spiritual way—perhaps—but——
Rachel You need to exercise your freedom, it's getting old and stiff, like mine. More freedom, more love, is what your book needs. (*She removes Bradley's tie*) Now kiss me again, just to prove you can.

Bradley kisses her

Bradley We must know what we're doing. I don't want to behave badly.
Rachel Who says anything about behaving badly?
Bradley (*pulling back a little*) You're not doing this to spite Arnold?
Rachel No. You're not just doing it to spite Christine?
Bradley Don't be crazy. Anyway I'm not doing anything.
Rachel Aren't you?
Bradley Could he have an affair with Christine?
Rachel I don't know, it doesn't matter. On that awful day—when he brought you in—as a witness—I might have hated you. But it's the opposite, I've *decided* it's the opposite. I've known you so long, and now—you've got a special role, like a knight with a charge upon him, my knight, my precious chivalrous knight.
Bradley You mean courtly love?
Rachel Yes.

As the conversation continues Rachel is pulling off Bradley's jacket, undoing the buttons of his shirt. She slips off her blouse

Bradley Rachel, courtly love isn't like this.
Rachel Are you afraid of Arnold?
Bradley Yes.
Rachel You mustn't be. I must see you unafraid. That's what being my knight is about. It will set me free, and it will set you free too. I've always seen you as a free spirit, a holy man, a wise man.
Bradley Well, I think this is most unwise. Moreover, I don't want it! We're both conventional middle-aged people.
Rachel I'm not conventional. That's what I've just discovered.
Bradley Well, I am. I'm pre-permissive. And you are my best friend's wife. Please do not start anything.
Rachel It's started. I do enjoy arguing with you.
Bradley You know where arguments like this end.
Rachel Yes.

They sit apart, staring at each other

SCENE 4

Bradley alone. He comes forward to the audience. He is holding a letter from Arnold

During the following reading, Bradley's flat becomes visible

Bradley I received a letter from Arnold. (*Reading*) "My dear Bradley, I have got into a mess and feel I must lay the whole matter before you. Christine and I have fallen in love. I know you don't believe in romantic love, but I assure you it exists. Of course I care for Rachel, but there is such a thing as simply getting tired of someone, our marriage is lifeless, almost a pretence. I have to look elsewhere. Of course I won't abandon Rachel, but I must have Christine too, and if that means running two establishments, well thank God I can afford it. I rely on you to help Rachel through this. Christine too needs something from you, your blessing on our relationship. Do you think you could see her soon and just say it's OK? Please? Arnold."

Julian enters. She carries a copy of Hamlet

(*Surprised*) Julian!

Julian You left the door open. It's terribly hot in here. You've forgotten. I've to come for my *Hamlet* tutorial. You said Tuesday was OK.

Bradley Did I? Oh dear.

Julian How is Priscilla?

Bradley Better. She's coming back here.

Julian Poor old thing, she must be *ages* older than you. Bradley, how nice to see you, you're so good for my nerves. Everybody irritates me like mad except you. Have you a moment?

Bradley Yes, yes.

They sit down opposite to each other at the table

Julian Bradley, this is fun!

Bradley Nothing's happened yet, it may not be fun.

Julian I'll ask questions and you answer—all right? I've got a whole list. (*She waves the list*)

Bradley All right, get on with it. I haven't got all day.

Julian (*reading from the list*) Why did Hamlet delay killing Claudius?

Bradley Because he was a dreamy scrupulous young intellectual who wasn't likely to commit a murder just because he imagined he'd seen a ghost. Next question.

Julian But isn't the ghost a real ghost?

Bradley Yes, but Hamlet doesn't know that.

Julian But there must have been another reason why he delayed, isn't that the point of the play?

Bradley I didn't say there wasn't another reason.

Julian What is it?

Bradley He identifies Claudius with his father.

Julian Oh, so that makes him hesitate because he loves his father and so can't kill Claudius?

Bradley No, he hates his father.

Julian But wouldn't that make him murder Claudius?

Bradley No. After all he didn't murder his father.

Julian I don't see how identifying Claudius with his father makes him not want to kill Claudius.

Bradley He doesn't enjoy hating his father. It makes him feel guilty.

Julian So he's paralysed by guilt? He never says so. He's fearfully priggish and superior. Look how nasty he is to Ophelia.

Bradley That's part of the same thing.

Julian How do you mean?

Bradley He identifies Ophelia with his mother.

Julian But I thought he loved his mother.

Bradley Yes, that's the point.

Julian How do you mean, that's the point?

Bradley He is furious with his mother for committing adultery with his father.

Julian Wait a minute, I'm getting mixed——(*She is trying at intervals to take notes*)

Bradley Claudius is identified with Hamlet's father on the unconscious level.

Julian But you can't commit adultery with your husband, it isn't logical.

Bradley The unconscious mind knows nothing of logic.

Julian You mean Hamlet is jealous? You mean he's in love with his mother?

Bradley That is the general idea. A tediously familiar one, I should have thought.

Julian (*after a pause*) Oh—that.

Bradley That.

Julian I see. (*Scribbling in her notebook*) I say, this is awfully interesting. Why couldn't Ophelia save Hamlet?

Bradley Because, my dear Julian, pure ignorant young girls cannot "save" complicated neurotic over-educated older men from disaster, however much they may kid themselves that they can.

Julian All right, I'm ignorant and young but I do not identify myself with Ophelia!

Bradley Of course not. You identify yourself with Hamlet, everybody does.

Julian I suppose one always identifies with the hero.

Bradley In great works of literature, not necessarily. Do you identify with Macbeth or Lear?

Julian Well no——

Bradley Or with Achilles or Agamemnon or Raskolnikov or Fanny Price or Madame Bovary or——?

Julian Wait, I haven't heard of some of them.

Bradley *Hamlet* is unusual because it is a great work of literature in which everyone identifies with the hero.

Julian Please—I want to catch up with my notes about Hamlet thinking his mother was committing adultery with his father—gosh, it is hot today—do you mind if I undress a little? (*She kicks off her shoes, pulls up her skirt, takes her jacket off, revealing a dress with narrow shoulder straps*) For this relief much thanks.

Bradley Do you mind if I take my jacket off? You'll see my braces.

Julian How exciting!

Bradley takes off his jacket and unbuttons his shirt a little. As he does so he frowns

Bradley Of course Hamlet is Shakespeare.

Julian Bradley, was Shakespeare homosexual?

Bradley Of course.

Julian Oh I *see* so Hamlet's really in love with Horatio——

Bradley Silence, girl. Life is serious, art is gay. Wittgenstein. Now if the greatest genius elects to be the hero of one of his plays, is this an accident?

Julian No.

Bradley So this must be what the play is about.

Julian What?

Bradley Shakespeare's own identity. When is Shakespeare at his most cryptic?

Julian The Sonnets?

Bradley Shakespeare is at his most complex and secretive when he's talking to himself. How is it that *Hamlet* is his most famous play, the best-known work of literature in the world?

Julian I don't know, you tell me.

Bradley Because Shakespeare by the sheer intensity of his meditation on the problem of his identity has produced a new language, a rhetoric of consciousness. Words are Hamlet's being as they are Shakespeare's.

Julian Words, words, words.

Bradley What work of literature has more quotable lines?

Julian To be or not to be that is the question.

Bradley Since my dear soul was mistress of her choice.

Julian Oh what a rogue and peasant slave am I.

Bradley For at your age the heyday in the blood is tame, it's humble, and waits upon the judgement. (*He is dismayed at happening upon these lines*) Something too much of this.

Julian Oh what a noble mind is here o'erthrown.

Bradley *Hamlet* is a monument of words, Shakespeare's most rhetorical and longest play. See how casually, with what easy grace he lays down the foundations of modern English prose.

Julian "What a piece of work is man"——

Bradley —"how noble in reason, how infinite in faculties, in form and moving how express and admirable, in action how like an angel, in apprehension how like a god!" *Hamlet* is a work endlessly reflecting upon itself, not discursively but in its very substance, a Chinese Box of words as high as the Tower of Babel, a mediatation upon the redemptive role of language. *Hamlet* is words and so is Hamlet. He is as witty as Jesus Christ but whereas Jesus speaks, Hamlet is speech. He is the tormented, sinful consciousness of man seared by the bright light of art, the god's flayed victim dancing the dance of creation. Shakespeare is prostrating himself before the author of his being, the god of love and art, the black Eros, the Black Prince, before whose countenance the unworthy shrivel like moths at a flame. Self-immolation, pure love, here invent language as if for the first time, changing pain into poetry and orgasms into thoughts. Shakespeare, *Hamlet*, *enacts* the purification of words, the deification of speech—we are redeemed because speech itself is ultimately divine——

Julian I played Hamlet once.

Bradley What?

Julian I played Hamlet once, at school, I was sixteen.

She smiles. Bradley staring at her, does not. She giggles

Bradley The show is over.

Julian Please—that was marvellous what you were saying—I want to write it down.

Bradley That stuff won't do for your exam. So you played Hamlet once. Describe your costume.

Julian Oh the usual. All Hamlets wear the same, unless they're in modern dress.

Bradley Do what I ask please.

Julian What . . .?

Bradley Describe your costume.

Julian Well, I wore black tights and black velvet shoes wth silver buckles, and a sort of black slinky jerkin with a low neck and a white silk shirt and a big gold chain and . . . What's the matter, Bradley?

Bradley Nothing.

Julian I enjoyed it ever so much, especially the fight at the end.

Julian poses a little, not looking at Bradley, imagining herself as Hamlet. Bradley stares at her

Bradley Here, thou incestuous murderous damned Dane!

Julian Yes—yes! Look, could you just tell me——

Bradley Enough, enough. How are your parents?

Julian You are a *tease*! They're all right. Dad's out at the library all day scribbling. Mum stays at home and moves the furniture about and broods. It's a pity she never had any education, she's so intelligent.

Bradley Don't be so bloody condescending.

Julian Sorry, that sounded awful, perhaps I'm awful, perhaps all young people are rather awful.

Bradley Lay not that flattering unction to your soul.

Julian I wish someone would write a really long nasty review of one of Dad's books, it might do him good.

Bradley So you want to be a writer.

Julian Yes, but not like that. And I won't call myself Julian Baffin!

Bradley Perhaps you'll be married then—and have—a different name— Julian, I think you'd better go.

Julian (*rising*) I've enjoyed this ever so much. Could we meet again? I
   don't want to be a nuisance. May I ring you?
Bradley All right. Off you go.
Julian You won't forget about me?
Bradley Go, go! Out!

Julian goes, leaving her copy of Hamlet *behind on the table*

(*He picks up the book and holds it to his face. Then he falls on his knees*)
Oh my God! (*He falls prone*)

Black-out

CURTAIN

ACT II

Scene 1

Bradley's sitting-room

Music

Bradley is revealed sitting in a chair, upright, quiet, composed, his hands folded, breathing deeply. He looks utterly serene, deeply happy. Priscilla's things are in evidence. Bradley muses softly

Bradley So. I am still alive. A thunderbolt struck me. But I am not destroyed. I am not desperate. I am not driven mad. I am driven sane. Lucid, truthful, redeemed. Saner than I have ever been. Stronger, wiser, better. I am setting my life in order. I have fetched Priscilla from the hospital and brought her here. I have brought back her things, all the things she wanted, her fur coat, her amber necklace, her silver looking-glass, her Chinese vases, her little animals. I shall look after Priscilla. I shall see Roger and Christine and Rachel and Arnold. I shall make peace in the world. It's all quite easy now.

The doorbell rings

Bradley goes and returns with Christine

Christine!

Christine (*defensively; holding up her hand*) Don't explode! I know you hate the sight of me!

Bradley I don't—I don't—I'm glad to see you!

Christine (*surprised, inspecting Bradley*) Oh, are you? You look all different. What is it?

Bradley I've just been over to Roger's place and got the things Priscilla wanted——

Christine Something's happened to you—you're beautiful, you're young. What have you been taking?

Bradley Oh, draughts of pure unilateral love—when you hope for nothing and you're just glad that something else *is*—like this vase. (*He brings out a ghastly vase of Priscilla's*) Isn't it marvellous?

Christine I don't know, but you've certainly improved.

Bradley The world is so beautiful—and if you can only stop thinking about yourself and think of somebody or something else, the beauty is everywhere, it crowds upon you, like swarms of golden bees. I am under a vow of eternal silence, but I am filled with love and on that I can live forever.

Christine Bradley!

Bradley He never told his love but let concealment—oh blessed concealment, womb of art, now wrapped in my cloak of darkness I shall write.

Christine Dearie me! Say, are you crazy?

Bradley Yes. No. I have achieved the higher sanity—absolute unselfish
love—it's unnnatural, it's terrifying, it takes you—out of yourself—
what's good, what's real is suddenly *somewhere else*—over there—and
you can *see* the whole world, everything that is, real and clear and
beautiful and full of light, like you've never really seen it before—
you're happy, you're free, you're pure in heart, you love everything!
And it's all there, all the things in the world, except for the one thing
that used to obscure the view—yourself—you have no self. The
disappearance of the ego is the secret of salvation. I am saved! Because
I love, and I want nothing in return. The only thing that can destroy the
self is absolute love.

Christine Are you in love with Jesus?

Bradley Yes, yes, Jesus too!

Christine My Zen teacher used to talk about destroying the ego, but I
never could, I guess I never wanted to. I think you'd better find that
analyst.

Bradley Chris, you were right about Priscilla, it was just a cry for help.

Christine Wait a minute. Did you notice something? You called me
"Chris" like in the old days. Who says there ain't no miracles?

Bradley I must tell you—I went over to get this stuff and Roger, you
know, her husband, has got his secretary installed.

Christine Oh my God.

Bradley Apparently she's been his mistress for years, she's called Marigold and she's pregnant—they were drinking champagne! No wonder
he wanted to get rid of Priscilla.

Christine Poor Priscilla—she always wanted a child. Better not tell her
just yet. (*She has been turning over Priscilla's things. She finds some of
them rather touching*) Oh, look.

Bradley By the way, I'm expecting Francis.

Christine You mean that foul crook Marloe!

Bradley Oh come!

Christine What's got you? You're all dewy and spiritual like a cat with
kittens. Bradley, did you get a letter from Arnold?

Bradley Yes—that's all right—I bless you—I bless you! (*He waves his
hand. He is now laying out Priscilla's possessions as listed in Act I, Scene
3, ready to surprise her*)

Christine Well—good—thanks. There's something I want to say, and
want you to say, that you forgive me, that there's peace between us.
When our thing went wrong I thought I'd be a cynic forever. When I
was in America the thing that really kept me going was money—not
painting or pottery or creative writing or analysis or Zen—only money
was real. And I was damn good at it, I'm a business woman. But I
always felt there was more to life, something higher, like a spiritual
dimension. I used to dream we were reconciled, you know, at night in
real dreams. And then I'd wake up and remember how we'd parted in

that awful crazy hatred. My God! And I felt when I was coming back here that I was coming for you, to you. And now—you know something—I feel you're open to me—I can walk straight in and there's *welcome* written on the mat. Brad, say those good words, say you forgive me, say we're reconciled, say we're real true friends.

Bradley Of course I forgive you, of course we're reconciled, of course we're friends, you see how easy it is.

Christine Yes, you're beautiful, you look like a god-damned saint. I never stopped thinking about you. After all, we were married in church, with my body I thee worship and all that jazz. You're a good man, Bradley Pearson. Let us open our hearts to each other.

Bradley Chris, dear, I——

Christine Kiss me, Bradley, the kiss of peace.

They kiss

Priscilla in a dressing-gown, enters and witnesses the scene. She suddenly sobs aloud

(*Going to Priscilla and kissing her*) Priscilla, darling am I glad to see you better.

Bradley Look what I've brought you——

Priscilla Oh, my fur coat.

Bradley —and all the things you wanted.

Priscilla My Chinese vases, my silver looking-glass. My little animals.

Doorbell

My amber necklace, my pearls.

Francis enters

Bradley Francis!

Priscilla My ducks!

Bradley Priscilla, here's your friend the doctor. Chris, you must be kind to Francis, he's been so good. Hasn't he, Priscilla? Isn't he a good egg?

Priscilla He is, he is!

Bradley Chris, say a kind word, you know how—he's your brother, he's my friend—I decree a season of good will!

Christine Bradley's gone mad, he's become a saint!

Francis Chris, don't be cross with me, dear——

Christine (*amused*) All right, come here, you rogue!

They shake hands

Bradley I'm so glad. Look, Priscilla, everyone's friends! Let's have a party, we'll celebrate. Give him a cheque, Chris, he's broke, give him a cheque, give him a cheque! (*He is becoming hysterical with euphoria. He produces sherry, hands drinks around*)

Christine (*laughing*) All right, all right! (*She produces her cheque book*)

Francis (*peering*) I say, could you make it five hundred?

Rachel enters. She looks with surprise at the festive scene

Bradley Rachel, my dear, I'm so glad you've come. We're giving a party, we're giving a party for Priscilla!
Rachel *Priscilla!* You're looking so well. What a lovely coat!
Christine Yes, isn't it just lovely.
Priscilla It's silver fox. Look, it's monogrammed!
Rachel (*amiably*) Hello, Christine.
Christine (*bad conscience*) Hello, dear Rachel.
Bradley Rachel, tell Arnold I'm going to read all his books again with a humble open mind!
Rachel Is Bradley drunk?
Christine No, he's just become good, maybe we should all try it!
Bradley Here's to Priscilla! Health and happiness!
All Priscilla, health and happiness!

Francis, clowning around, puts on some earrings and a hat

Francis Bradley, won't you sing to us? Chris, you remember how Brad used to sing?
Christine Yes, come on, Bradley.
Bradley We'll all sing. (*He sings*)
          Great Tom is cast.
          And Christ Church bells ring
          One, two, three, four, five, six
          And Tom comes last.

Bradley sings first alone, then conducts the others to sing in round. The round soon gets hopelessly mixed up and they go on singing and laughing. The scene darkens a little. Music, a cacophonous medley of the tune joins the voices, the voices fade as the singers are lost in darkness

    Francis, Priscilla, Christine and Rachel exit

Bradley is left alone, holding his head. The horror of the situation has reached him at last. The music gradually changes, the stage lightens

SCENE 2

The same

Bradley is alone

Julian enters

Julian I left my book.

Bradley hands it to her. Another pause

Bradley I'm just going away. So I must say goodbye.
Julian I—I felt I wanted to talk to you again. (*She puts the book down*)
Bradley (*laconic, abrupt*) So sorry, I'm off to the country. I'll be away some time. Francis is coming to look after Priscilla.

Julian I'm sorry you're going. I wanted to thank you.

Bradley That's kind of you. Now I'm afraid I have a train to catch. (*He looks at his watch*) I mustn't keep you. (*He goes to the telephone*)

Julian Don't be cross with me.

Bradley I'm not cross with you.

Julian (*upset, near to tears*) Yes, you are. You're being cold, and hostile. You know how much I like and admire you. I just wanted to see you.

Bradley Thank you for coming. I'm sorry to be in such a hurry. I just can't see you—I—I don't want to see you.

Julian Why? There must be a reason. (*Pause*) And I think I know what it is.

Bradley (*handing her* Hamlet) Don't forget your book.

Julian Bradley, I know—because of the way you looked at me last time, and the way you're behaving now.

Bradley If you want me to gratify your vanity by a display of my feelings you will be disappointed.

Julian You are displaying your feelings.

Bradley Why have you come here to bother me?

Julian I wanted to be sure. Don't you want to talk about it?

Bradley No, of course not. There's nothing to talk about.

Julian This concerns me too. I'm upset too. You have upset me. You speak as if there was no-one involved but you.

Bradley There is no-one involved but me. You're just something in my dream!

Julian I'm not, I'm real, I'm here. Don't you care what I think?

Bradley (*with bitter amusement*) My dear Julian, of course I don't care what you think! Now please run along, there's a good girl. I'm just going to ring for a taxi.

Julian No you're not.

They stare at each other

Bradley You're a criminal.

Julian Don't you think that you can hurt me—don't you think that I can suffer?

Bradley Suffer? You!

Julian You're just concerned about yourself. All right, I'm concerned about myself. You started it. You can't just stop it now when you decide.

Bradley The fact that I may imagine myself to be in love with you does not preclude my knowing that you are a *very silly girl*. This thing is not a toy, your curiosity will be unsatisfied and your vanity unflattered. And I hope that, unlike me, you will *keep your mouth shut*.

Julian Don't be like that, please talk to me. Don't you want to talk to me about your love?

Bradley No. I imagined talking to you about it. But that was in the fantasy world. I can't talk love to you in the real world. What do you want me to do—praise your eyes?

Julian Has telling your love made your love end? It hasn't, has it?

Bradley No. But it has no speech—any more—its tongue has been cut out.

Julian You talk as if there was nobody here but you.

Bradley There is nobody here but me.

Julian So you don't want to know what I feel.

Bradley I know what you feel. You are amused and pleased because an older man is making a fool of himself.

Julian How old are you Bradley?

Bradley (*slight hesitation*) Forty-two.

Julian (*slightly shaken*) Oh—forty-two—well, I don't call that old. Bradley, don't be so horrid to me. (*She reaches out a hand*)

Bradley I may be a fool, but that's no reason for you to be a bitch.

Julian To a nunnery go, and quickly too——

Bradley (*pointing to the door*) Farewell!! (*He goes to the telephone*)

Julian It doesn't occur to you that I might return your love.

Bradley (*removing his hand from the telephone*) No.

Julian I've known you all my life, I've always loved you. I was so happy when you came to see my father and I could ask you things and tell you things—so many things weren't real at all until I'd told you them—you were a sort of touchstone of reality to me. If you only knew how much I've always admired you. When I was a little child I used to say I wanted to marry you. Do you remember. All right, you don't! You've been my ideal man for ever and ever. This isn't just a silly child's thing, it's real deep love, of course it's a love I haven't questioned or thought about or even named until quite lately—but now I have questioned it and thought about it—now that I'm grown up. You see, my love has grown up too. I've so much wanted to be with you and know you properly— since I've been a woman. Why do you think I wanted to discuss *Hamlet*? I did not want to discuss *Hamlet*, but I much more wanted your affection, your attention, I wanted to *look* at you. I've *longed* to touch you and kiss you in these last years, oh years, only I didn't dare to, I never thought I would. I've been thinking about you all the time—I love you, I love you.

Bradley I'm not accusing you of insincerity, just of not having the faintest idea what you're talking about. *Don't touch me!*

Julian advances. Bradley retreats. She seizes his sleeve. He wrenches it away. She stands before him. They stare at each other. Then he quietly takes her into his arms and they embrace, eyes closed, without kissing. Then Bradley thrusts her away

You little devil.

Julian I love you.

Bradley Don't talk lying rubbish.

Julian Why do you think it's impossible? Do you think I'm a child, or that you're so unlovable?

Bradley Both. Oh Julian, I intended to lock this thing up until it died of starvation. And now—we mustn't do this. You are younger than you think, I am older than you think.

Julian I'm in love with you. I've been *trembling* since I last saw you. I had to come and see you. I feel absolutely shatttered and yet I feel absolutely calm. I feel like an archangel. Oh, please kiss me, please.

They kiss, briefly

Bradley God. Let's sit down.

They sit down on the sofa

Julian We aren't doing anything wrong.

Julian begins to unbutton Bradley's shirt. Bradley removes her hand. Perhaps he is uneasily reminded of a recent similar scene

Bradley We mustn't be together, we mustn't see each other——
Julian I so want to touch you, it's so marvellous, it's a privilege. (*She gently touches his face, drawing her fingers down*)
Bradley You're mad.
Julian Bradley—dear—don't be afraid. We'll just get to know each other slowly and quietly, tell each other the truth and tell each other everything and look—and look—and——
Bradley All right, Julian, we'll talk—we've got to talk each other out of this!
Julian If we talk—we'll talk each other—deeper in—deeper and deeper—in.
Bradley (*in panic*) You mustn't feel tied, there's no tie, there's no connection, we mustn't define this, we mustn't use words like "love"——
Julian Don't be silly——
Bradley I'm terrified.
Julian I'm not. I've never felt braver in my life. I haven't said anything to my parents of course, I couldn't till I was sure, but I'll tell them now.
Bradley *What?* What'll you tell them?
Julian That I love you and I want to marry you.
Bradley Julian—it's impossible—this is a dream—it's even a lie——
Julian Bradley, it's true, it's truest, it's the test of all truth.
Bradley I'm too old.
Julian Lots of girls prefer older men—you don't just want a love affair and then goodbye?
Bradley No!
Julian Real love is forever.
Bradley Yes, I know—but, Julian, don't—I'd rather you didn't tell your parents.
Julian You think they won't like it?

SCENE 3

Bradley's flat. Arnold's house

Bradley and Arnold are talking by telephone. Rachel with Arnold, is listening on the extension

Arnold Bradley, get back to reality. You're in some sort of dream world. You're nearly sixty. Julian is twenty. She said at the start that you'd told her your age and that she didn't mind, but you can't mean to take advantage of a sentimental child who is flattered by your attentions——

Bradley She's not a child.

Rachel She's a child!

Bradley I didn't want her to tell you.

Arnold You asked her to deceive her parents?

Rachel I think he's really in love with Christine, and he's subconsciously transferred it to Julian.

Arnold *Is* it Christine?

Bradley No! I don't care *what* Christine does! Thank you for your letter, by the way!

Arnold All right. You find Julian attractive. But if you felt randy about her, why the hell didn't you keep it to yourself, instead of annoying and upsetting her?

Bradley She's not annoyed or upset.

Arnold She was this morning.

Bradley Then you upset her. You evidently don't know what it is to be in love. Now I come to think of it, you've never really described it in any of your beastly novels!

Arnold What *you* imagine about your vile feelings and lusts is your affair. Julian is certainly not in love.

Rachel (*seizing the telephone*) You haven't been to bed with her, have you?

Arnold (*taking the telephone back*) Of course he hasn't, he's not a criminal!

Bradley I haven't. Please don't get angry—you're frightening me—I'll leave her free—she *is* free—but I can't say I won't see her.

Arnold If you pester her now, you'll make an *emotional situation*, that's what you want, and that's what I won't allow. Now I hope you'll have the decency to leave London at once!

Bradley You don't understand. I am not proposing to go away.

Arnold What do you propose to do?

Bradley Stay here, see Julian a bit—get to know her—since it appears we love each other——

Arnold Bradley! I warn you! I will take any measures to stop this.

Bradley Don't be so angry, I haven't done anything wrong.

Rachel (*taking the telephone*) Yes, you have. You spoke to her about your feelings. And you permitted yourself to *have* such unspeakable feelings!

Bradley Rachel——

Rachel (*softly*) You have behaved horribly, and I will never forgive you.

Rachel disappears

Arnold (*continuing*) By the way, that letter I wrote you, there's no need to do anything about it just now.

Bradley I wasn't going to.

Arnold It's not unusual for men of your age to want to sow some unsavoury wild oats. I'm going to take Julian away and you won't know where she is. I'm going to hide her until you come to your senses.

Julian enters Bradley's flat. She is carrying a suitcase

Bradley Oh, so you're going to hide her . . . and I won't know where she is . . . oh dear.

Arnold Hello . . . hello . . .

Bradley replaces the telephone and embraces Julian

Arnold replaces the receiver and goes

Julian Oh Bradley, whatever shall we do?

Bradley (*his joy fading*) I don't know. (*He points to her suitcase*) What's that?

Julian I've left home—oh it's been such a *nightmare*.

Bradley I gather they weren't pleased.

Julian I was a perfect idiot. I told them all about it last night in a triumphant sort of way—I've never seen my father so angry, he got quite violent, he shook me——

Bradley Oh my dear child——

Julian And then I lay on my bed and couldn't stop crying. And later on they said they'd rung you and you'd agreed it was all nonsense and you'd said you were going away.

Bradley That wasn't true, of course.

Julian I knew it wasn't, and I wouldn't promise not to see you and then the row started again and my father was shouting and my mother was crying and I *screamed*, and—I just didn't know ordinary educated middle-class people could behave like we behaved last night!

Bradley That shows how young you are! I wish it wasn't open war—you *can't* be certain, you ought to be locked up—it'll end in tears.

Julian Then this morning they were pretending to be nice and reasonable, and I said I quite understood and I'd got over it, and then I crept out the back way.

Bradley Oh my heroine, but darling, what do we do now? They'll be here.

Julian We'll run.

Bradley But where to?

Julian Anywhere, to a hotel.

Bradley We can't go to a hotel, we haven't anywhere to go. MY GOD, YES WE HAVE! We can go to my cottage, my secret cottage beside the sea! (*He telephones*) Can I have a taxi, please, to go to King's Cross Station? . . . Pearson. You know, Penrose Court. Straight away? . . . Thank you.

Priscilla enters. She is dressed ready for departure, with handbag and fur coat

Priscilla Hello, Julian. Bradley, I've decided to go back to Roger. You were quite right. We should forgive each other and be reconciled. Could you send my things on after me?

Bradley starts to conduct Julian and her suitcase out and then returns

Bradley Priscilla, you can't go back, you can't!
Priscilla Why not!
Bradley (*frantic, almost shouting*) Because Roger has got somebody there, he's got a mistress, they've been together for years, they've settled in the house, it's their house now, you can't go back any more! Oh God, I'd forgotten all about you—Francis said he'd come—Roger's mistress is there—she's called Marigold and she's pregnant.

Priscilla sits down. She speaks very slowly

Priscilla She's pregnant. You mean Roger and his mistress have taken it all over, it's theirs now?
Bradley Yes!
Priscilla Did you see them?
Bradley Yes—she's young and beautiful, they're happy, they're in love——
Priscilla I was thinking of Roger all alone, all by himself, trying to cook something in the kitchen, missing me, wanting me, and feeling sorry he'd been so bad——
Bradley He's not sorry! They're singing and drinking champagne! You can't go back, Priscilla, it's too late!

The doorbell rings

Julian, hold the taxi.
Julian Is Priscilla all right?
Bradley Yes, of course.

Julian goes out, taking her suitcase

Priscilla You're on their side. Everyone is on their side. God is on their side. You'd forgotten all about me.

Francis enters

Bradley Oh it's you, thank God. Francis said he'd stay here and look after you. I'm just going away. I'll ring you later. (*He rushes to his suitcases*)
Priscilla Bradley, don't go away, don't leave me!
Francis What about the money? The *money*?
Bradley I'll give you a cheque. (*He tears out a cheque and gives it to Francis. To Priscilla*) You'll be all right, Francis is here.

The doorbell rings

Francis (*frantic; waving the cheque*) Brad, sign the cheque! Sign it, quick, just sign it!
Julian It's the taxi.

Bradley scribbles his signature

Priscilla Bradley——!
Bradley Coming!
Priscilla Don't go, don't leave me. I'll kill myself!

Bradley rushes out with suitcases

Francis gloats over the cheque, finds the sherry bottle and pours out two glasses. Priscilla is crying. He sits with an arm around her, offers her a glass which she thrusts away

(*More softly*) I'll—kill—myself.

Francis No, you won't. It's a bad world. I don't like it either. It's a bloody rotten lousy cruel old world. Full of tears, oh the oceans of our tears. All we can do is try to cheer ourselves up. Come on!

She accepts the glass

SCENE 4

The sitting-room at Bradley's cottage

A brilliant scene, large windows, sunlight. Bradley is heard singing his liberation song

Julian enters, then Bradley, carrying towels, also stones, shells, bits of wood. Julian is holding a sheep's skull. Bradley and Julian have been transformed into outdoor seaside people, Bradley in shorts, Julian in bathing costume with colourful robe. They have been swimming, then exploring the beach. Julian holds up the skull

Bradley Memento mori.

Julian What? It's a sheep's skull, isn't it? Look, it's so smooth and shiny, like ivory. The sea has made it into a work of art.

Bradley It's a symbol of death, a beautiful beautiful symbol.

In spite of his words, Bradley is clearly very happy. Julian begins to arrange the stones

Julian Stop it, darling. We've been swimming, we've been in paradise.

Bradley We've become angels, not saints, angels.

Julian We can hear the sea. Listen.

No sound

Bradley No we can't, it's too calm—and it depends on the wind.

Julian We heard it last night. Didn't we hear it last night?

Bradley We did, we did!

Julian This has been the happiest day of my life. A long perfect day. Don't worry about Priscilla. We'll have her to live with us.

Bradley We won't be living anywhere. There isn't any future. Don't think I'm complaining. He lives eternally who lives in the present.

Julian Of course there's a future! I've bought brown bread, and toothpaste, and a saucepan, and an axe for chopping wood.

Bradley Yes. But they're like the fossils religious people said God planted when he created the world in 4000 BC to give us an illusion of the past.

Julian Bradley——

Bradley We have an illusion of the future.

Julian Don't talk in that silly way, it's a way of lying!

Bradley We have no language in which to tell the truth about ourselves.

Julian I have, I'm going to marry you! We're free, we aren't married to anyone else. Think what a bit of luck that is! And you're going to write a great book. Look, here are your notebooks! (*She displays them*)

Bradley So white, so pure . . .

Julian Bradley, you're tormenting me, you say bad things on purpose.

Bradley Perhaps, but I must *move* a little, even cause pain, if I am to apprehend you at all. Yet I feel so connected with you, I *am* you, I've never *been* another person like this before——

Julian We've only just found each other.

Bradley We found each other millions and millions of years ago.

Julian Then we're safe.

Bradley I don't doubt your love, my darling, I'm grateful for it on my knees.

He kneels and kisses the hem of her robe. She raises him

It's just that whatever miracle made us will automatically also unmake us. We are for breaking. Smash is what we're for.

Julian You say these awful mechanical things because you're afraid to be happy.

Bradley Yes, I fear the gods.

Julian Look at these beautiful shells and stones, this piece of wood with the funny pattern on it, they prove something.

Bradley Priscilla thought her fur coat and her amber necklace and her pearls proved something.

Julian We'll look after Priscilla and make her happy. Darling, don't reject happiness. I'll keep you here till you learn it!

Bradley It's not my subject. I'm no bloody good, that's the trouble.

Julian I know what's worrying you, it's last night, and this afternoon.

Bradley Well, yes. That was a failure. I mean I was a failure.

Julian You weren't a failure. You held me in your arms and I was perfectly happy—I've never been so happy in my life.

Bradley It's like not being able to write, the god isn't there, he just isn't there.

Julian He'll come—and you'll be able to write too. Dear heart, don't grieve, it will all come right.

Bradley God, how I love you. But it's no good, I'm old, I'm older than you think.

Julian Nonsense, look at yourself, you're young, you're beautiful. Bradley Pearson, will you marry me?

Bradley Julian——

Julian Will you marry me, yes or no?

Bradley You're quite mad! I am your slave, and whatever you go on wanting will be the law of my being.

Julian Then that's settled and you can stop boring me about your age!

Bradley For all that beauty that doth cover thee is but the seemly raiment

of my heart, which in thy breast doth live, as thine in me. How can I
then be older than thou art?
Julian Is that a quotation?
Bradley It's a damn rotten argument.

*Silence. Pause. They embrace. The scene darkens a little, faintly reddish
glow, twilight. They now speak softly, enchanted*

Julian Bradley, it's midsummer. Shall we go down and look at the sea?
Bradley A midsummer night's dream—-no—stay here, my sovereign lady.
Julian How absolutely we've come home. Haven't we?
Bradley Yes. If we can only stay here a bit longer, we're safe—forever—
perhaps. (*Pause*) Look, there's the evening star.
Julian We're inside a huge magic palace which reaches as far as the stars,
as far as the outer galaxies, as far as——
Bradley Dangerous places, magic palaces.
Julian You mean they tend to vanish? But we're magic too—it's our
magic. Wherever we are is magic.
Bradley Julian, thank you for this perfect time. Nothing can damage this
or take it away, ever, it's something eternal.
Julian Sing to me, Bradley, I've heard you sing for other people, you've
never sung just for me.
Bradley (*singing*)
> Full fathom five thy father lies,
> Of his bones are coral made,
> Those are pearls that were his eyes,
> Nothing of him that doth fade,
> But doth suffer a sea-change
> Into something rich and strange.
> Sea-nymphs hourly ring his knell
> Hark! now I hear them,
> Ding-dong bell.
> Hark! now I hear them,
> Ding-dong bell.

Pause after the end of the song. The scene darkens a little more

Julian Thank you. All's well. (*She rises, ready to go into the bedroom*)
Come soon.
Bradley Yes.

Julian exits

*Left alone, Bradley goes to the table where his writing materials are laid
out. He picks up a notebook*

Yes. Love is the discovery of what one has always known. Art is the
discovery of what one has always known—and which alone is true—
locked into place by the dance of viewless atoms and the vast
revolutions of the cosmos. I thought my poor sad patience would have
to live its whole life without reward. But now—my love releases my art,

my art enables my love. Like a magician who has waited ten thousand years for the juxtaposition of two stars, I have waited for this moment.

He raises his hands in prayer and triumph, then moves restlessly, tormented by joy and fear. He finally goes towards the bedroom door. The telephone rings. Bradley leaps to pick it up. He speaks softly throughout the conversation

Hello. Yes, it's me. Who's that? . . . Francis! How did you know where I was? . . . What? What's the matter? Has Arnold found out? . . . Francis, what is it? . . . *What* about Priscilla? . . . Oh God—Oh no—what——? . . . Sleeping pills. . . . It can't be, it's another false alarm, she can't be dead. . . . Oh . . . No, it's my fault. Oh God. . . . All right, stop moaning. Tell me how you found out where I was. . . . I see. Does Arnold know I'm here? . . . No-one knows but you? . . . . Hold on, just keep quiet for a moment, I want to think. (*He covers the mouthpiece. He looks at the bedroom door. Silence. He uncovers the mouthpiece*) Look—don't tell anybody where I am or that you got in touch. . . . No, I can't come back. . . . Yes, yes, she's my sister, but I can't come back yet. I will come. . . . It was only an accident that you found the estate agent's letter. You must consider that this telephone call did not happen. . . . Roger can fix the funeral. Do whatever you'd do if you couldn't find me! . . . Oh—why did you leave her alone? . . . Oh stop—do as I tell you. There's nothing we can do for Priscilla. She isn't there any more. (*He puts down the receiver, sits with head in hands, moans quietly*)

> *After an interval Julian emerges from the bedroom. She has put on her Hamlet gear, black tights, black jerkin, gold chain, white shirt, etc.*

She poses, holding the sheep's skull in one hand. Bradley, after a moment, lifts his head and sees her

Julian Oh! that this too solid flesh would melt, thaw and resolve itself into a dew.

Bradley What are you doing?

Julian What do you think? Don't I look like the Prince of Denmark? Don't stare so. What's the matter?

Bradley Nothing.

Julian I brought this stuff to please you. Bradley, you're frightening me. What is it?

Bradley Nothing.

Julian I'll take it off—don't be cross——

Bradley (*rising*) I'm not cross.

Julian (*still frightened*) Bradley, darling——

Bradley Oh—Julian——

He seizes her, tries to pull off her jerkin, gets entangled in the chain. Julian struggles to help him to remove the jerkin, unbutton the shirt

Julian Don't be so rough, you're hurting me!

Bradley (*sobbing*) It's the god—oh how terrible—Oh Julian . . .

He buries his face in her hair, then picks her up and carries her into the bedroom

The music of the song is heard, first soft, then triumphant, then dying away into the sound of the sea as the stage becomes dark

SCENE 5

The same

Darkness. Then a terrible knocking at the door. Silence. Then more knocking

Bradley in dressing-gown with electric torch, emerges cautiously from the bedroom, followed by Julian in nightgown

Julian (*whispering*) What is it?
Bradley I don't know.
Julian Who can it be?
Bradley You stay inside.
Julian Keep quiet and don't put the light on, they'll think there's no-one here. Oh I'm so frightened.

The knocking begins again. A metal object is pounding the panels of the door, there is a sound of splintering wood

Bradley Stay in the bedroom and lock the door.
Julian No, no, Bradley, don't let them in!
Bradley Stay in there!

He pushes Julian back into the bedroom and shuts the door

He turns on the lights. Silence. He opens the door

Arnold enters. He puts the axe he is holding on the table

Arnold (*almost speechless with rage and emotion*) Is Julian here?
Bradley Yes.
Arnold I've come to take her home.
Bradley She won't go. How did you find us?
Arnold Francis told me. And about the phone call.
Bradley What phone call?
Arnold He telephoned you last night and told you about Priscilla. You couldn't drag yourself away from your love-nest, even though your sister had killed herself!
Bradley I'm coming to London and Julian is coming with me—we're going to be married.
Arnold The car is outside. I want my daughter.
Bradley No.
Arnold Where is she? (*He moves towards the bedroom door*)

Bradley picks up the axe. He opens the door and speaks through it

Bradley Your pa is here. Don't worry. We'll just explain the situation and see him off.

Julain enters. She is dressed, jeans, shirt

Arnold (*controlling himself*) My dear——
Julian Hello.
Arnold I've come to take you home.
Julian This is home.
Arnold You can't stay with this man. Here's a letter from your mother. Please read it.

Julian automatically takes the letter

We've been so terribly worried—how could you be so cruel, staying here—and after what's happened to poor Priscilla.
Julian What about Priscilla?
Arnold (*triumphantly*) Hasn't he told you?
Bradley Priscilla is dead. She killed herself with an overdose of pills.
Arnold He knew last night. Francis told him by telephone.
Bradley That's correct.
Julian You didn't tell me—and we were—in there——
Arnold Aah!
Bradley There was nothing I could do for Priscilla. But for *us*—I had to stay—it wasn't indifference.
Arnold Lust is the word. Don't you see what he is?
Julian (*in tears*) Bradley, how awful, how could you, oh poor poor Priscilla—and we wanted to make her happy!
Arnold He is totally callous. His sister dies and he won't leave his foul love-making.
Bradley I was going to tell you, and then we'd go to London. Please *listen*. I felt if we could only stay a little longer—here—alone—we'd be bound together forever. Do you understand? We needed this piece of time, *this* piece of time. I said nothing because of *you*, because of our love——
Julian Oh Bradley——
Bradley We'll go back now, together, and—oh I'm so much to blame!
Julian It was my fault, because of me. Otherwise you'd have been with Priscilla, she begged you to stay. It's happened because of us—why didn't you say when Francis phoned?
Arnold The sexual gratification of an elderly man. *Think*! He's thirty-three years older than you.
Julian No, he isn't he's only forty-two.
Arnold (*triumphant laughter*) He told you that, did he? He's fifty-three.
Julian He can't be.
Arnold Look him up in *Who's Who*.
Bradley I'm not in *Who's Who*.
Julian Bradley, how old are you?

Bradley Fifty-three.

Arnold When you're thirty he'll be a pensioner. Isn't that enough? Let's go, Julian, you can have your cry in the car.

Julian Are you really fifty-three?

Bradley Yes, Julian.

Arnold Can't you see he is?

Julian Yes I can—now.

Bradley You said you didn't mind what age I was.

Arnold Come along, Julian.

Bradley You can't *go* suddenly just like this, I've got to talk to you properly——

Arnold I am very upset and very angry and I am trying hard to be reasonable. I will not leave without you. Consider your mother's feelings. *Read her letter.*

Julian, distracted, tears open the envelope and holds the letter

Bradley I want to explain to you——

Julian How can you explain!

She begins to read the letter. Bradley, still holding the axe, bars the door

Bradley My darling, don't leave me, don't leave me, I shall die—I can't let you go, I'll go mad, stay with me——

Arnold Can't you see it's *over*? You've had a caper with a silly girl and now it's *finished*, the spell is broken.

Julian is clearly upset by the letter

Bradley Julian, we haven't lost each other, have we? I'm so deeply sorry I lied about my age, I did it instinctively—but it doesn't really matter, does it? And about Priscilla, I *had* to stay with you and be with you—I've done everything because I love you.

Julian is in tears

My darling, my love, let's sit down and talk quietly together, we'll talk about how it will be, how we'll be happy, and we'll go to sleep in each other's arms and everything will be all right.

Julian I can't stay here—I must go home with my father.

Arnold Thank God.

Bradley Don't go—stay with me! (*He moves forward*)

Arnold seizes Julian and pushes her out of the door

(*Rushing after them; shouting*) Julian! Julian!

SCENE 6

Bradley's flat

The sunny weather is over. The window is dark. Priscilla's things are visible, untidly piled together

Francis and Christine, with umbrellas and mackintoshes. They gradually take off their macs and shake the umbrellas. They are in mourning. They exchange glances, looking at the door

Christine Who was the poetry by that the man read? (*Getting no answer, louder*) It was such a lovely service. Who was the poetry by?
Bradley (*off*) T. S. Eliot.
Christine Was he Priscilla's favourite poet?

No answer

Francis Brad, I'll stay with you here if you like.
Christine He'd better come round to my place.
Francis He'll want to stay here because of—you know—might turn up.
Christine You could stay here and—Bradley, you'd better come over and stay at my house for a while. Francis could hold the fort here.
Bradley (*off*) No thanks.
Christine You need looking after.

No answer

I'll pack Priscilla's things and send them back, you needn't worry.
Francis Can't Brad keep them?
Christine No. That swine Roger actually came up to Bradley at the funeral and of course he was Priscilla's heir and not to forget the silver fox! (*She holds it up*) I guess it'll just fit Marigold. (*She begins to sort and tidy the pile of clothes and ornaments*)

Bradley enters. He sits on the sofa

Bradley (*tonelessly*) There's another bag under the stairs.
Francis I'll get it. And I'll put these in the kitchen.

Francis goes out carrying the umbrellas and macs

While he is away Christine approaches Bradley

Christine (*softly*) Brad. It's your old Chris—I do so much want to help.

Bradley smiles faintly, does not take her extended hand

Francis comes back with the bag

Christine begins to pack it, wrapping ornaments carefully up in clothing. Francis sits down beside Bradley, trying to attract his attention

Francis Brad, I wasn't out for long, I swear, I just met this chap in the pub like I said, and he kept on talking.
Bradley Yes. You told me.
Francis Then later on I tried to wake her up——
Bradley You told me.
Francis I don't see how I can go on living—Brad, you do forgive me, don't you?
Bradley Yes, yes.
Christine Oh brace up, Francis, stop whining, leave the poor sod alone. What did Rachel say when you went round?

Bradley She said Julian was away somewhere with Arnold.
Francis I'll look for her. I'll find her!
Bradley He's holding her by force, she's a prisoner, as soon as she escapes she'll come here.

Francis and Christine look at each other and shake their heads. Poor Bradley is deluded. The doorbell rings

   Bradley, galvanized into frantic activity, rushes to open it

(*Off*) Rachel!

Bradley returns with Rachel

Christine Why it's Rachel. Hello Rachel I hope you're well.
Bradley Rachel——
Rachel Hello Christine.
Bradley —where's Julian?
Rachel Bless you, I'm so glad you're looking after her.
Christine Thanks dear.
Bradley Where's Julian?
Christine Come on Francis, let's be somewhere else.
Francis I want to stay here.
Christine Francis, come on!

   They depart

Rachel (*calm, dignified*) I wanted to tell you how sorry I am about Priscilla.
Bradley *Rachel, where's Julian?*
Rachel On holiday, with Arnold, I told you!
Bradley She can't be, she's a prisoner, where is she?
Rachel I should imagine somewhere in the Lake District.
Bradley The Lake District!
Rachel They went off by car. Julian loves a trip.
Bradley A trip!
Rachel Here are the letters you sent her, by the way, I haven't opened them. (*She hands Bradley several letters*)
Bradley She'll come back to me as soon as she can get away.
Rachel Bradley, she left you of her own free will. Poor old thing, you look terrible, you look a hundred. Calm down, it's all your fantasy.
Bradley You didn't think so when Julian said she loved me.
Rachel Your Julian is a fiction, it's all a mistake. You make me sick! Not so long ago it was *me* you were kissing passionately! Remember?
Bradley Nothing happened. I made it perfectly clear I didn't want it. I can imagine you may feel resentful——
Rachel Resentful! It was just feeling sorry for you. And if nothing happened it wasn't because you didn't want it to! Our liaison was entirely for your benefit.
Bradley There was no liaison!
Rachel Well, I suppose it didn't last long. No wonder Julian could hardly believe it.

Bradley (*staggered*) *You told* Julian?

Rachel Yes, of course. I told Arnold at once how you'd sprung upon me, he was most amused. He suggested I write a letter to Julian about our relationship. He thought it might be an effective argument!

Bradley (*appalled*) That letter——

Rachel Naturally she came running back to hear all about it, so I told her.

Bradley What did you tell her?

Rachel Everything, it would have been wrong to conceal it.

Bradley Oh, God!

Rachel Bradley, one is responsible for one's past actions and you can't blot them out by entering a dream-world, you can't make yourself into a new person overnight, however much in love you feel you are. Do you really imagine you would be the final resting-place of a young girl's passion? Her final choice?

Bradley *What did you tell her?*

Rachel I think you're having some sort of nervous breakdown. I told her about us.

Bradley What did she say?

Rachel What could she say, poor child, she was crying like a maniac.

Bradley What?

Rachel She got me to repeat it, give the details, swear it was all true and she believed me.

Bradley What did she say? Can't you remember anything she said?

Rachel She said "If only it had been longer ago." I suppose she had a point.

Bradley You misled her, you lied to her!

Rachel Bradley, don't shout! She'd already seen it was a silly mistake. You're a lonely frustrated man, and you may have misunderstood my little attempt to help you. I'm afraid happily married couples sometimes make victims of people they're sorry for. Arnold and I tell each other everything, we laugh about it, we're very happy together.

Bradley (*dazed*) I thought Arnold was going off with Christine, he told me he was——

Rachel Don't be crazy!

Bradley My mind's going—I thought he wrote . . . (*He goes to the writing-table and takes out Arnold's letter and reads from it*) "Christine and I have fallen in love——"

Rachel snatches the letter and reads it

Rachel You did this on purpose.

Bradley I'm sorry, I didn't know what I was doing, I'd *forgotten* about it. He doesn't mean it.

Rachel God you're vile, vindictive!

Bradley You said you and Arnold told each other everything.

Rachel You're a dangerous horrible person, living in a dream, breaking everything, wrecking all the happiness you can't have. No wonder you can't write, you aren't really here at all. Julian looked at you and made you real for a moment, I made you real for a moment because I was

sorry for you. Now all that's left of you is a crazy spiteful ghost. I shall
hate you forever. You kept this letter as a weapon against me.

Bradley Honestly, Rachel, I haven't given you a single thought!

Rachel Aaaaaaaaarrgh!

*Rachel turns away and runs out screaming. Her screams gradually die
away*

Red light on stage

Bradley (*litany*) I'll make a wager with the god. I'll give it up.
            Let these blank pages not be written on.
            Forget my prayers, let there be no book.
            Only let Julian come back again.
            I here unmake all that I meant to do.
            All that I ever begged for I hereby surrender.
            Only let her come back, and love me, as she said.

*Bradley tears up his notebooks. The telephone rings, he rushes to it in a
frenzy*

Julian! . . . Oh, it's Rachel. . . . Is Julian there? . . . What? Is Julain
all right? . . . What's the matter. . . . You've done *what*? I can't hear.
. . . Yes, yes, I'll come round.

Bradley rushes out

SCENE 7

The sitting-room at Arnold's house

*The room is wrecked as in Act I, Scene 2. Chairs overturned. The bookcase
shows a conspicuous gap. Arnold's books have been torn up and scattered
on the floor. The periodical with Bradley's review of Arnold's latest novel
lies upon the table*

*Arnold's body, sprawling on the sofa, is reminiscent of Rachel's in Act I,
Scene 2. Rachel is sitting moaning*

Bradley enters

Rachel points towards Arnold. Bradley kneels to look

Bradley Oh my God!

Rachel (*whispering*) He's dead.

Bradley Yes—I think so—oh Rachel . . . (*He rises. He picks up the
bloodstained murder weapon; the familiar poker, which is lying nearby*)
You did it—with this . . .

Rachel He's dead—he's dead.

Bradley What happened?

Rachel I was so angry, I started to tear up all his books, he tried to stop
me. I hit him—we were arguing, shouting—I didn't mean to—he
started screaming with pain—I couldn't bear it—I hit him again just to
stop him screaming.

Bradley (*with the poker; frantically*) We must hide this, you must say it was an accident—oh what shall we do—he can't be dead—Arnold! Arnold! Did you ring for the doctor?

Rachel He's dead—I killed him——

Bradley Did you ring the doctor—ambulance—police?

Rachel No.

Bradley It was an accident—he fell and hit his head—that's what happened—I'll clean this up and—no fingerprints . . . (*He takes a handkerchief from his pocket, carefully cleans blood and fingerprints off the poker, and pockets the handkerchief again. He keeps hold of the poker*) I hope that disposes of—we ought to clear up this mess—Rachel, I'm going to telephone—remember it was an *accident*.

Rachel It's no good—no good . . . (*She rocks to and fro in anguish*)

Bradley (*confused, distraught*) You must say it was an accident—or—or—self-defence! He hit you first, and you—Rachel, please *think* what you're going to *say*!

Rachel Oh my darling, oh my love, oh my love . . .

Bradley dials 999

Bradley Hello, emergency, someone badly hurt, ambulance, police—Milford House, Kent Gardens—my name is Pearson—yes—yes—Rachel, they're coming, remember, it's not your fault—oh . . .! (*He picks up the poker which is now once more stained with blood*) It's all bloody. God, I ought to—clean all this up . . . (*Still holding the poker he tries ineffectively to tidy the scene*)

The sound of police sirens

Rachel, for God's sake think what you're going to tell them!

Three Policemen enter

They observe the scene, inspect the body. One, moving in and out of the room, occupies himself with Rachel, who sits sobbing incoherently

I'm afraid there's been an accident. I think he's dead. He fell and hit his head. He's Arnold Baffin, the writer. This is Mrs Baffin.

1st Policeman And who are you?

Bradley My name is Bradley Pearson, I'm a writer too.

2nd Policeman (*at the body*) Stove his head in. (*He takes the poker from Bradley*) Thank you, sir.

Bradley You won't find any fingerprints on that except mine. Oh dear, there's more blood on it, I dropped it on the floor.

Bradley takes out his bloodstained handerchief and wipes the end of the poker. The 1st Policeman takes the handkerchief from him. The 2nd Policeman has picked up the periodical from the table and shows it to the 1st Policeman

2nd Policeman Did you write this article, "Arnold Baffin, The End, We Hope"?

Bradley Yes, but that's not my title. I wouldn't have used that title, the
editor put it on, editors are always doing that.

*The 1st Policeman points to the books on the floor which the 2nd
Policeman has been examining*

1st Policeman Who tore up these books?
Bradley I did—I mean—(*more softly*) no, not these ones actually . . .

*The 3rd Policeman, tending Rachel, has been at the door, talking to those
outside*

3rd Policeman Mrs Baffin, we've just got your daughter on the phone,
would you like to speak to her?
Bradley Julian!
Rachel He killed my husband.
3rd Policeman Come along now.
Rachel He murdered him.
3rd Policeman Don't worry, we'll look after you.
Rachel (*sobbing as she goes with the 3rd Policeman*) He's dead, he's dead.
3rd Policeman Come along, we'll help you, gently now.

He leads Rachel out

1st Policeman I think you'd bettter come along with us, Mr Pearson. It is
my duty to warn you that anything you say may be used as evidence
against you.
Bradley You don't think I killed him? I didn't kill him, I didn't! He was
my best friend. (*He stands appalled, silently apprehending his situation*)
1st Policeman Come along please, Mr Pearson.

EPILOGUE

Bradley, Rachel, Francis, Christine and Julian

Bradley The Great British Public absolutely loved my trial. Everyone
including my lawyer, believed I had killed Arnold. *Writer slays friend
out of envy.* Of course I never stood a chance. Arnold's books,
supposedly torn to pieces by me, were brought into court in a tea-chest
and fingered by the jury. I think that was what impressed them most. As
for Rachel, all she had to do was dress in black and mop her eyes. There
was a reverent sigh whenever she entered the box. It never entered
anyone's head that she could have any motive for killing her husband.
Marriage is a very private place.
Rachel I do not want to be unkind, even to the murderer of my husband,
but since Bradley Pearson's fantasy life has achieved some notoriety I
feel that I must speak. Bradley was not an artist—he was an unhappy
disappointed man who pretended to be an artist. He claimed to be a
perfectionist but he never wrote things and tore them up. I'm sure he
never tore up anything except my husband's books. We all regarded
him as an absurd little man, a figure of fun, someone one couldn't

mention without smiling. He must have realized this. That's a shocking thought that a man might commit a serious crime just because people laughed at him. He was obsessively envious of my husband—and he knew that my husband really despised him. That must have caused him continual torment. Of course the romance with my daughter was pure fantasy. He was actually deeply in love with me. How far that unrequited passion led him to commit such a terrible deed it is not for me to say.

Bradley My life sentence gave general satisfaction. It was a mean contemptible crime, to kill your friend out of envy of his talents. And poor Priscilla, rising from the grave, pointed her accusing finger. My "callous indifference" to her death, which the defence said proved me insane, in effect proved me a monster. Perhaps you will say that the judgement was not entirely unjust. Of course—my extreme love—for that girl—did in some sense occasion the deaths of both Arnold and Priscilla. We cannot altogether evade responsibility for the chains of moral failure which bring about the evil which we protest that we never intended.

Francis It is not for me to dispute the sentence passed upon my friend Bradley Pearson—but as a man of science it is my duty to explain his conduct. We have here the classical symptoms of the Oedipus Complex. Male children love their mothers and cannot forgive them for having sex with their fathers. So, many adult men detest women. It's as simple as that. Bradley is obviously a homosexual as I demonstrate in my forthcoming book *Hamlet, Or the Case of Bradley Pearson*. He appeared to be in love with a girl—but look! He falls in love when he imagines her as a man, he achieves sexual intercourse when she is dressed as a prince. And who is Bradley's favourite author? The greatest homosexual of them all, William Shakespeare! What is Bradley's favourite fantasy? Boys pretending to be girls pretending to be boys. And who is this girl anyway? The daughter of Bradley's rival, friend, enemy, *alter ego*, Arnold Baffin. Artists adore themselves, their attachments to other people are always unhappy. Bradley was blessed, or cursed, with only one genuine attachment. Perhaps I should not instance his attachment to myself as evidence of his sexual tendencies. But may I take this opportunity of saying to my old friend—I was aware of his feelings, and I valued them highly.

Christine I want to say how very sorry I am for poor Bradley. He didn't mean to kill his friend, he did it in some sort of mad brainstorm. His memory of our marriage isn't all that clear either—we never hated each other, I just got bored! I wasn't surprised to find he'd got nowhere and done nothing, I was even a bit pleased—isn't that awful? I wanted to help—I guess it was just curiosity really. When I turned up all rich and joyful of course he fell for me all over again and I had to throw him out a second time—and that's what made him go crazy. All his family were a bit off, his mother was a monster, and his sister could have used some electric shocks. And his mania about art, as if it were religion! We can live without art I should think—what's so special about art? Maybe it's some consolation if you *imagine* you're an artist. I hope Bradley's not too miserable in prison. Perhaps it's a blessing to be insane if it makes you think you're happy when you're not.

Julian I find it difficult to identify myself with the child who imagined she loved Bradley Pearson. Perhaps there was such a child, and perhaps it was me. I never read Pearson's writings. There was something impressive there, a lifetime of trying and failing. It seems brave to go on trying. It also seems stupid. I am a writer myself now, a poet. I favour a small but perfect product. Pearson was wrong to picture some god as the ruler of art. Art is cold. Especially when it portrays passion. Erotic love never inspires good art. Love is concerned with possession. Art is concerned with truth. Pearson was not cool enough. He wanted to be the victim of a dark power, but there is nothing there. Art has no master.

Bradley (*sitting*) The soul, seeking its survival, looks into the darkness. I lost my Julian. But I wrote my book. (*He takes a book out of the table-drawer and stands*) I have changed my beloved into art. I have preserved her inside this frame. (*He gestures to indicate the prison, the theatre*) This is her immortality—from this embrace she cannot escape. So speaks the artist. And yet, my dear, dear girl, however passionately my thought has worked upon your image, I cannot really make myself believe that I invented you. At the last you evade me; art cannot assimilate nor thought digest you. I do not know or want to know anything of your present life. Yet elsewhere, I realize, you are, you laugh, you cry, you walk in the sunlight, read books, perhaps write books, lie down in someone's arms. May I never deny this knowledge, or forget that it was a real person that I loved so much. That love remains, altered but undiminished, a great pure love with a clear memory. It causes me remarkably little pain. Only sometimes at night when I think you live now and are somewhere, I shed tears.

CURTAIN

FURNITURE AND PROPERTY LIST

ACT I

SCENE 1 (Bradley's flat)

On stage: Sofa. *On it*: folded rug
Writing-table. *On it*: telephone, telephone directories
Chairs
Cupboard. *In it*: bottle of sherry, glasses
Two suitcases

Personal: **Bradley:** wrist-watch (worn throughout)

SCENE 2 (Arnold's house)

On stage: Sofa
Table. *On it*: bottle of whisky, glasses, novel, telephone with extension
Overturned chairs
Bookcase. *On shelves*: some books
Books strewn on the floor
Waste-paper basket

Off stage: Towel (**Francis**)
Bottle, glasses (**Arnold**)
Bottle, glasses (**Francis**)
Cassette player with headphones, letter (**Julian**)

Personal: **Francis**: address on piece of paper

SCENE 3 (Bradley's flat)

On stage: As Scene 1

Set: Arnold's novel on writing-table

Off stage: Glass of salt water (**Bradley**)

Personal: **Priscilla**: handbag containing a bottle of pills
Bradley: letter, book review

SCENE 4 (Bradley's flat)

Strike: Priscilla's handbag
Used glasses
Arnold's novel
Rachel's jacket and blouse

Re-set:	Bottle of sherry in cupboard
Off stage:	Copy of *Hamlet*, notebook, pen, list (**Julian**)
Personal:	**Bradley**: letter

ACT II

SCENE 1 (Bradley's flat)

On stage:	As Act I, Scene 1
Set:	Priscilla's silver fox fur coat
	Earrings
	Pearls
	Amber necklace
	Small ornaments including ducks and little animals
	Chinese vases
	Silver looking-glass
	Various items of clothing including a hat
Personal:	**Christine**: handbag containing a cheque book and pen

SCENE 2 (Bradley's flat)

| *On stage:* | As previous scene |

SCENE 3 (Bradley's flat/Arnold's house)

On stage:	Bradley's sitting-room: as Act Scene 1
	Arnold's sitting-room: table. *On it*: telephone with extension
Off stage:	Suitcase (**Julian**)
Personal:	**Priscilla**: handbag
	Bradley: cheque book and pen

SCENE 4 (Bradley's cottage)

On stage:	Chair
	Table. *On it*: notebooks, paper, pens, telephone
Off stage:	Sheep's skull, towel, stones (**Julian**)
	Towel, shells, bits of wood (**Bradley**)

SCENE 5 (Bradley's cottage)

On stage:	As previous scene
Off stage:	Practical torch (**Bradley**)
	Axe (**Arnold**)
Personal:	**Arnold**: letter

Scene 6 (Bradley's flat)

On stage:	As Act II, Scene 1
Re-set:	Priscilla's items in an untidy pile together on the floor
Set:	Bag Letter in drawer of writing-table Bradley's notebooks
Off stage:	Wet umbrellas (**Francis, Christine**) Bag (**Francis**) Several letters (**Rachel**)

Scene 7 (Arnold's house)

On stage:	Sofa Overturned chairs Bookcase. *On shelves*: books arranged around a conspicuous gap Books torn and scattered on the floor Table. *On it*: tray with bottle of whisky, glasses, a periodical Bloodstained poker near sofa
Personal:	**Bradley**: handkerchief

Epilogue

On stage:	Chair Table. *In drawer*: book

LIGHTING PLOT

Property fittings required: nil
Three sitting-rooms

ACT I, SCENE 1

To open: General lighting, sunshine effect from window
No cues

ACT I, SCENE 2

Cue 1	**Bradley**: "And it's not the end of that either." *Fade to spot on* **Bradley**	(Page 5)
Cue 2	**Bradley**: ". . . until you are amazed at your luck." *Crossfade to general lighting*	(Page 5)
Cue 3	**Bradley**: "That's a secret!" *Fade to spot on* **Bradley**	(Page 9)

ACT I, SCENE 3

To open: General lighting, sunshine effect from window

Cue 4	**Priscilla**: "Oh, I'm so *frightened*." *Fade to spot on* **Bradley**	(Page 10)
Cue 5	**Bradley**: ". . . so it didn't signify." *Crossfade to general lighting with sunshine effect from window*	(Page 10)

ACT I, SCENE 4

To open: Spot on **Bradley** downstage

Cue 6	When ready *Bring up general lighting on Bradley's sitting-room*	(Page 21)
Cue 7	**Bradley** falls prone *Black-out*	(Page 25)

ACT II, SCENE 1

To open: General lighting, with sunshine effect from window

Cue 8	As they all continue singing and laughing *Reduce lighting slightly*	(Page 29)
Cue 9	Music: a cacophonous medley *Fade to spot on* **Bradley**	(Page 29)
Cue 10	The music gradually changes *Gradual increase to overall lighting*	(Page 29)

ACT II, SCENE 2

To open: General lighting, with sunshine effect from window
No cues

ACT II, SCENE 3

To open: General lighting on two sitting-rooms

Cue 11   **Bradley** replaces the receiver   (Page 34)
            Fade lighting on Arnold's house

ACT II, SCENE 4

To open: General lighting, with brilliant sunlight through windows

Cue 12   They embrace   (Page 38)
            Reduce lighting and bring up faintly reddish twilight glow
                through windows

Cue 13   Pause after the end of the song   (Page 40)
            Reduce lighting further

Cue 14   Music dies away into sound of the sea   (Page 40)
            Fade to black-out

ACT II, SCENE 5

To open: Darkness

Cue 15   **Bradley** turns on the lights   (Page 40)
            Snap on general lighting

ACT II, SCENE 6

To open: General lighting, with dull grey day effect from window

Cue 16   **Rachel**'s screams gradually die away   (Page 46)
            Crossfade to red lighting

ACT II, SCENE 7

To open: General lighting

No cues

ACT II, EPILOGUE

To open: Lighting on **Bradley**

Cue 17   **Bradley**: "Marriage is a very private place."   (Page 48)
            Spot on **Rachel**

Cue 18   **Rachel**: ". . . it is not for me to say."   (Page 49)
            Fade spot on **Rachel**

Cue 19   **Bradley**: ". . . that we never intended.   (Page 49)
            Spot on **Francis**

Cue 20   **Francis**: ". . . and I valued them highly."   (Page 49)
            Crossfade to spot on **Christine**

Cue 21   **Christine**: ". . . you're happy when you're not."   (Page 50)
             Crossfade to spot on **Julian**

Cue 22   **Julian**: "Art has no master."   (Page 50)
             Fade spot on **Christine**

EFFECTS PLOT

ACT I

Cue 1	**Bradley** (on the phone): ". . . Thank you." *Doorbell*	(Page 1)
Cue 2	**Francis:** ". . . all sins forgiven." *Doorbell*	(Page 2)
Cue 3	**Bradley:** "No! Go away!" *Telephone*	(Page 2)
Cue 4	**Rachel** departs *Pause, then distant door slam*	(Page 5)
Cue 5	**Bradley** (on the phone): ". . . Thank you." *Doorbell*	(Page 9)
Cue 6	**Priscilla**: ". . . she's dead, she's DEAD." *Doorbell*	(Page 11)
Cue 7	**Bradley:** ". . . miss my train." *Doorbell*	(Page 11)
Cue 8	**Priscilla** gags *Doorbell*	(Page 11)
Cue 9	**Francis:** "Not at all, it was a pleasure." *Doorbell*	(Page 13)
Cue 10	**Bradley**: "No." *Ambulance arriving*	(Page 13)
Cue 11	**Bradley** reaches for the telephone *Telephone*	(Page 19)

ACT II

Cue 12	To open *Music; fade when ready*	(Page 26)
Cue 13	**Bradley:** "It's all quite easy now." *Doorbell*	(Page 26)
Cue 14	**Priscilla:** "My little animals." *Doorbell*	(Page 28)
Cue 15	The scene darkens a little *Cacophonous medley of tune as script; when ready, change music and then fade*	(Page 29)
Cue 16	**Bradley:** ". . . it's too late!" *Doorbell*	(Page 35)

Cue 17	**Bradley**: ". . . Francis is here." *Doorbell*	(Page 35)
Cue 18	**Bradley** goes towards the bedroom door *Telephone*	(Page 39)
Cue 19	**Bradley** carries **Julian** into the bedroom *Music of the song, then fading into sound of the sea*	(Page 40)
Cue 20	To open Scene 5 *Loud metallic knocking at door; silence then more knocking*	(Page 40)
Cue 21	**Julian**: "Oh I'm so frightened." *Knocking begins again, sound of splintering wood*	(Page 40)
Cue 22	**Francis** and **Christine** shake their heads *Doorbell*	(Page 44)
Cue 23	**Bradley** tears up his notebooks *Telephone*	(Page 46)
Cue 24	**Bradley** tries ineffectively to tidy the scene *Police sirens*	(Page 47)